The H

G000241984

Steven Gordon was born and brought up in Roehampton. He was educated at film school and spent several years working in television. In 1998, he graduated from Cambridge University and now lives and works in North London. *The Happy Room* is his first novel.

Steven Gordon

The Happy Room

Acknowledgements
Thanks to Dr Anneke Westra for checking my biology,
Dr Lyall Watson and his many publications for inspiring it and
Beth Shaw, Roger Keeling, Sue Nash, Amber Jones and Jeff Phelps for
putting up with it for so long. Also special thanks to Carol Bowen whose
encouragement made this book possible.

This edition published in Great Britain in 1999 by
Allison & Busby Limited
114 New Cavendish Street
London W1M 7FD
http://www.allisonandbusby.ltd.uk

A catalogue record for this book is available
from the British Library

ISBN 0 7490 0426 6

Cover design by Neil Straker Creative

Printed and bound in Great Britainby
Biddles Ltd, Guildford and King's Lynn

To Peggy and Jack

If a chair is a *sign*, wheels on that chair are a *signifier*.
– Ferdinand de Saussure

1. For Starters

Random Thoughts And Themes – what I did as a small child which still sticks in my mind. Staring at things like a piece of silver paper because I thought it was fascinating. Thinking that jumping on the settee in my socks was a really good thing to do. Realising that sleeping in the garden in a tent made out of blankets was the best thing that could ever happen to anyone.

As I bumped the chair off the pavement, jerked it into gear and accelerated, the rough-terrain tyres squealed – the top speed of the average motorised wheelchair was about 15mph, mine would do 55mph, that's because its 105cc Suzuki engine was fuel-injected and super-charged.

It was 7.30am and the estate was full of morning sounds – fizzing radios, slamming doors, cars starting up. As I roared past Hilsea Tower a woman scraped birdshit from her Vauxhall's windscreen and as I flashed passed Portsea House a man emerged coughing and buttoning his coat – all very *rise and shine*, all very *let's get cracking*. Then a breeze hauled slowly across the square ticking every leaf in the line of horse chestnut trees and I swerved, juddered the chair to a halt, pulled out my notebook and began to scribble fast.

I recognised the rhyme scheme – or rather the lack of one – immediately. It was an idea I'd been working on for some time, and after a minute or two I read it out aloud –

      ALIVE
      her mouth
      is the adventure of my lips

and the orbit of her face
the turn of my heart

we sleep for years –
and shit on the pretenders
the dialogue of glass –
martyred oaks –
mountains –
it all burns
even the colours of the day

I was really pleased! I'd come to love these off-the-cuff/scratch-card type poems, much better than agonising for ages over every phrase or word. In celebration, I gunned the chair and veered down the road doing a wheelie.

Precious moment over, I turned out of Wanborough Drive and crossed Roehampton Lane, where at the junction with Alton Road I came to a police road block. I slowed and bumped up the pavement. In the middle of the junction, surrounded by a wagon-train of emergency vehicles, two cars had meshed together head-on as if they'd tried to eat each other. A young couple had gone through the windscreen of one car and were bloodily splayed across the bonnet and in the second the mangled corpse of a middle-aged man sat with a steering wheel neatly embedded in his chest. I killed the chair's motor and watched as paramedics began to gently prise the bodies from the wreckage. Why do people throw away their lives like that? Why is it that when they get behind the wheel of a car all their caution and reason seem to fly out the window? Of course, it could be down to the gadget itself, for since the 1890s the car has killed nearly fourteen million people worldwide. That's quite something isn't it? Fourteen million dead because someone invented a self-propelled box on wheels. Not nearly as good as the helicopter – only three thousand four hundred and sixty-eight dead since its debut in 1937, or the electric trouser press – just one victim since 1959.

For some reason we seemed to get a lot of car accidents in and around Roehampton at that time. Or perhaps it was just me getting paranoid. Yet I did have an excuse for worrying, as a road accident had killed my mother, put my sister Evangeline into a PVS coma and broken my spine in three places. This is the story of how that happened and what happened afterwards. Call it a life story if you like. A sort of autobiography, with the oomph on auto.

2. The Double Bubble Café

Random Thoughts And Themes – kindness. Taking two bottles to a party. Kissing someone whose breath stinks like a toilet, but not letting on. Always telling a friend the truth, even though the poor bastard will probably top himself when he hears what you have to tell him.

After ten minutes of the crash scene, I'd had enough, so I cruised down to the Double Bubble Café for breakfast.

Finances permitting, I ate at the Double Bubble nearly every day because it was the best café in Roehampton and I was a good friend of Maurice, the owner. I chained the chair up outside, got out my crutches, pushed at the door – and there was an empty café.

'I know – where is everybody?' said Maurice. Who was quietly standing behind the counter frying some bacon. 'Actually, I've only just opened up.'

'Overslept?' I said

'No, car wouldn't start.'

'Cars again!'

'And have you heard about the smash on Alton Road?'

'Saw it on the way over ...'

'What a waste. What a terrible waste ...'

'When you've got a moment, Maurice, I'll have beans, mashed potato, two slices and a tea, please ...'

Awful crash scenes aside, this was a typical breakfast for me as I never ate cereals and only had fry-ups on very special occasions. Which was hard, because I loved them – the stark sun-like egg, the slender, crinkly curves of bacon, the glinting semi-spheres of tomato. Food, as you're going to find out, is one of my favourite subjects. Incidentally, did you know that the word Food is one of the six most commonly used words in any language? But from then on things become complicated because its exact meanings vary from culture to culture. It's easy, of course, to poke fun at the eccentric examples – Guyanese poached coypu's stomach, Moroccan diced doves' gizzards, etc. But what really fascinates me are the darker sides to culinary choice and taste, those areas that hint at strange inner confusions, which when investigated seem only to throw up further difficulties. More of this later.

My meal arrived. This had taken Maurice all of two minutes to organise. Maurice was not only an excellent cook, he was also incredibly fast.

'You're a one off, Mo,' I said.

Maurice grinned and pressed his big doughy belly against the counter.

'I know you don't want to hear this,' he said, 'but I'm really pissed off at the moment.'

'The course?' I said, trying to sound enthusiastic, because I knew what was coming. Maurice was doing an MSc in Cooking As Therapy at Thames Valley University. It had been a good idea to start with because he was genuinely serious about counselling, but the course was not what it was cracked up to be, so he was now running out of steam with it.

'Guess what I'd really like to do?'

I shook my head.

'A research degree in prosthetics.'

'A research degree in prosthetics?'

'I really fancy it.'

'What would the thesis be about, exactly?' I said, coyly.

'A History of Prosthetic Facial Features – the ivory false palate of a French courtesan; the golden nose of a Rajasthan maharaja; the quartz iris of a Shogun prince. That sort of thing.'

Prosthetics was a sort of hobby of Maurice's. He'd once shown me a photograph of a false leg made out of impacted chewing gum. Apparently, this had been found attached to the thigh of a strangled San Franciscan cinema manager. Maurice had a vast collection of such black curiosa.

'Sounds interesting,' I said. 'What are the chances of converting?'

'Nil.'

'Really?'

'They're not going to let me convert from cooking to prosthetics are they? I'd need a new faculty, a new supervisor, a new everything.'

'Still, if that's what you want to do. They *might* let you convert. Anything's possible. Why don't you ask?'

But Maurice – suddenly in a mood – turned away, punched open the water urn's gas handle and slowly the café filled with the sound of boiling water.

I know this is going to sound a bit off the wall, but I've always found the sound of boiling water special. It touches something deeper in me somehow, linking with other similar sounds that calmly bubble in my memory, but again, more of this later.

When I'd finished eating I sat quietly gazing out of the window, thinking about that couple from the car crash. I wondered how long they'd known each other and who would remember them. Yes, that was vital – who would remember that dead boy and girl? Just then a man walked past the café window who looked like Vile. He had the same dark-eyed, fiendish, I-am-a-psycho look. Yet as he crossed the road, I got a good look at him and no, it wasn't Vile. Close though.

'Any faults, Maurice?' I said, leaning back in my chair.

Maurice was cracking eggs onto the griddle.

'There's no hurry but on COMMANDO, the ball sometimes sticks in the soldier's brain and on KILLER-GRANNY at stage 25, the Granny won't leap across the chasm.'

For a second or two I watched the eggs that Maurice was cooking balloon like huge boils on the hot griddle, then I got out my tool bag from behind the counter.

At the rear of the café, a pinball and two video machines stood in a row. COMMANDO was the very pinnacle of pinball technology at that time. The baseboard was a three-D, rippling impression of an Arnold Schwarzenegger type cradling a massive bazooka. I unlocked the machine and shone my pen-torch inside. Sometimes dust would build up in a niche and retard a circuit. And sure enough, a fleck of polystyrene was lodged near a contact. I poked it with my screwdriver and it fell into my hand. Then I gave the PCB boards a wipe and moved across to KILLER-GRANNY.

'Mo, who took KILLER-GRANNY to stage 25?'

Maurice was now flipping sausages on the griddle. They spun in the air like tiny acrobats.

'Have you seen that little girl that comes in here sometimes? You know, the one with the limp and the thick-lensed specs?'

Swiftly, I took KILLER-GRANNY to stage 25. Yet strangely, I couldn't find anything wrong. I pressed on to stage 30 and still had no problems. I concluded that a glitch, which had somehow cleared itself, had made the Granny baulk at the bottomless chasm at stage 25. She didn't baulk at anything with me though. On the contrary, she jumped the chasm, skilfully machine-gunned the pedestrians in the streets and fire-stormed the city most efficiently. Though at stage 32, I did have some trouble getting her into the hospital to knife the patients in their beds, but this could have been the odd slow finger reaction on my part, it's difficult to say.

3. The Block

Random Thoughts And Themes – things that are squalid. Levering out ear wax with a finger and then flicking it. Playing with phlegm in your throat by making realistic coughing sounds. Scratching yourself and finding it too satisfying.

Fifteen minutes later, at the junction with Danebury Avenue, I swung out into the south-bound traffic, jinked into the outside lane, slammed into fourth and left everyone for dead. As I did so a red BMW in the middle lane nudged the bumper of the car in front. That never failed to amuse me – *the shocked traffic factor*. But then I suppose being cut up by a wheelchair for a BMW owner, is a shocking thing in a way.

At the Alton Road junction, things were getting back to normal. The two crashed cars were being towed away and only two policemen were left measuring the scene and taking notes. I bounced up on the pavement before they saw me and accelerated hard towards the common.

I visited the common almost every morning – what with the fresh air and peace and quiet – it really was the high point of my day. But that morning, I was preoccupied with my poison arrow lizards.

My PAL's were a particularly tricky behavioural trial I'd been working on – I was attempting to train them not to poison their adversaries. Yet old habits die hard and so sometime during the previous night, one of them had killed his aquarium neighbour, a yellow wolf spider. It was a problem. I coasted the chair to a halt opposite Scio Pond, got out my sticks and slid down the side of the embankment.

At the pond's outlet, a mizzle of flies speckled a bar of sunlight. It had been a good summer and the common was heavy with growth. There were even orchids growing in some of the quieter corners. The outlet poured from a pipe about 4ft in diameter. This was an excellent habitat for all kinds of animals – voles, toads, newts, even bats. Carefully, back bent, I edged inside.

To see where I was going, I held my pen-torch between my teeth and to keep my balance, pressed my head against the brick roof. It stank of piss and shit in there, but then those places always do, don't they?

At that time, I was very keen to build up a collection of *Pipistrellus pipistrellus* bats, for *pipistrellus* have some social habits that I was anxious to monitor. Yet as usual, all of my six bat traps were empty. The trouble with bats is that they are very accurate flyers and seldom bump into things. Particularly traps.

Next I checked my mousers.

These traps were dotted along the banks of the stream under various bushes and trees, and as was nearly always the case, were full. At the final count, I had two dormice, two field mice, a young water rat, a shrew and a weasel.

Without fuss I jarred all of these, except the weasel, because he was legs-in-the-air. Weasels have very high metabolic rates, so a combination of rage and panic had probably given this one a heart attack. Yet I cut his head off with my sheath knife and carefully bagged it all the same, for local animal brain and teeth stats were of particular interest to me.

Lastly, I checked the insect collectors.

These were also full. Earwigs, centipedes, lacewings, dungflies, loads and loads of craneflies and two extremely beautiful ghost swift moths. I collected insects mainly for my carnivorous flora, so I was pleased with the glut of craneflies, as they were a favourite food of my finicky *Sarracenia lenco-phylla*. But I was saddened by the ghost swifts, as the female of the pair was in oestrus, yet dead. This was a shame, for ghost swifts are not common in South London. Yet moths have an extraordinary sense of smell, as a male can track a female from a range of over 30 miles using just one molecule of her scent, so this pair had probably come up country from the south coast where they were more plentiful. Gently, I plucked the male from the gauze of the trap, blew his wings down and straightened a crease or two. He was weak, but with a nudge lifted slowly into the air.

I went back to the chair, packed everything neatly in the saddle bags and took off for the estate.

It was a lovely warm day with a light breeze blowing and for some reason I felt happy. I looked up – in the distance stood the massive finger-like shape of Witley Tower. Awesome! But minutes later, as I slewed around Wanborough Drive, I came face to face with the Cape.

The Cape – dressed like something out of a DC comic – had been hanging around Witley for months, scaring dogs and old ladies. As I watched, he slid from the second floor of Witley and slipped into the bushes by the playground. I had to stifle a laugh – it could only happen here. I stared up at the building, its immense parallaxes bowed gently like a gigantic vase and as I slotted my card-key into the wall dispenser there was a whirling sound, a click, the front door opened and a blast of hot air hit me full in the face. Due to faults, Witley's central heating system had been on most of the summer, so the block was like a greenhouse. In fact it was so hot and feisty in there that germination and regeneration were going on everywhere – sedge and grasses sprouted on stairways, algae and mould fuzzed the windows and I'd even come across a wooden bannister that was budding!

I parked the chair on the ground floor, removed the rotor arm, and took the lift to the sixth floor.

'VILE! IT'S ME – DEAN!'

I squinted through the letter box. I could smell something nauseous and hear the sound of a dog snarling, which were good signs, as they meant that Vile was in. Suddenly a wild-looking eyeball thrust itself against the spyhole. I smiled cheesily at it and immediately the chubbs began snapping back.

'All right?' said Vile, standing in the doorway, grasping Claire by her studded collar.

Claire, a 10-stone toza, sniffed at my trousers, recognised me, clasped one of my legs with her front paws and began to wank hard.

'GET DOWN!' shouted Vile, 'GET DOWN!!'

I'd known John De Vile all my life. He and I were cousins on my mother's side – the De Vile side, that is, which came down through a Norman knight who was a friend of the Percys, or something. About two years before the time I'm writing about, Vile was thrown out of university and needed somewhere to stay. Witley was perfect. He'd begun a chemistry degree at college but halfway through had discovered that he could earn hundreds of pounds a day by making and selling hallucinogenics. So on the face of it, he barely survived at university on a mandatory grant, but was actually living off campus like a king with his own two-bedroomed flat, a sound system to rival Knebworth and a water bed so large you could dip sheep in it as well as count them. Yet three years on he was a much less flamboyant character. A couple of heavy busts concluding in twenty-one months inside Wandsworth Prison had seen to that.

'What's this?' I said.

We were standing in Vile's tiny lab, where on a bench a tangerine-coloured liquid was distilling from a flask.

Vile grinned. 'My latest smack sub. It's based on a trychrine-methadone compound. Try some?'

'Is it any good?'

'Best sub I've ever designed.'

We sat outside on the balcony. The view this side of Witley Tower was Richmond Park, Kingston and the Thames. But that day, behind the park, a heat haze hung like a wall, obliterating everything beyond.

'I haven't done any S for ages,' I said.

'Then this is the dream for you,' said Vile, handing me a polka-dot capsule.

'Polka-dot?'

'As a matter of fact it's a very friendly marking which quite a few insects use. The South American bark beetle, for example, has polka-dot receptors and antennae ...'

I swallowed the capsule, chased it down with a sip of Sprite and then stared out into the colourless sky.

'Ever played Subbuteo?' said Vile.

'When I was about eight. Why?'

'I was thinking about it last night. Brian and I started a league. It was good. We had over two dozen kids in it at one time.'

'The set we had was totally naff, half the players were missing.'

'Did you see the Subbuteo championship on Channel Four?'

'Subbuteo on the telly?'

'They filmed it in Italy, but the action replays were shit ...'

'What's Brian up to these days?'

'He's working for a demolition company in Leicester.'

I smiled.

'Do you remember his Airfix kits?'

'Do I?' said Vile. 'For years I went to sleep each night with a pair of Messerschmitt 109s swinging six inches from my face.'

'I remember my first Airfix – a Hawker Hurricane.'

'I made three before I realised that if you unfolded the paper that the plastic bag was attached to, there were instructions. I hated that – having instructions. Did you do the dinosaurs?'

'I didn't know Airfix did dinosaurs.'

'They were excellent. What about the armies?'

'Oh, yeah – Afrika Korps, Roundheads, Cavaliers ...'

'Brian and I made these mutants. We'd pull the tail-plane off a bomber and glue it onto the back of a car. Or pull the guns from a warship and stick them all over a lorry.'

'Weird.'

I smiled and closed my eyes. I felt good. Slowed. It was curious, but I had the sensation of the s-sub gently soaking into my brain. Which I suppose is exactly what it was doing.

'I've started the Opium Garden again,' said Vile.

'What?'

'The Opium Garden. Down in the basement.'

'Oh, the Opium Garden.'

'I've planted the whole of basement 4 with poppies. I'm telling you, Dean, I've got plants down there nearly six feet tall!'

All at once, I felt my eyes popping and for some reason I couldn't close my mouth. Vile looked at me and laughed.

'Your face!' he cried.

'What?'

But Vile couldn't stop laughing and suddenly that's all he was – one vast, laughing mouth balanced on a chair.

'You know, this time we're going to do the whole thing differently,' said the massive mouth. 'No street scenes. No hello officer. We're going into mail order. We're going to sell the best skag in Europe by post.'

'Mail-order drugs?' I said. 'But what happens if the police trace back to the base address?'

A huge tongue licked huge lips.

'The police won't have an address to trace back to – we'll do everything by mobile. And there's no way they'll be able to trace the numbers, as they'll all be linked to ficti-tious clients.'

'Fictitious …' I said, carefully probing the word with my tongue. 'Fictitious,' I repeated, suddenly stroking syllables which were now hard and erect.

4. The Facts

Random Thoughts And Themes – things that I've seen fall from the sky, the memory of which, for some reason, has stayed with me ever since. A dead blackbird in my friend Alan Nicholson's back yard. A tiny lizard which fell at my feet while on holiday in Greece. A fucking great chunk of wood that smashed into the windscreen of the car I was travelling in one windy Sunday morning on the way to Sea Scouts.

Due to the Moon's tidal drag the duration of a day varies. This is calculated to be increasing at a rate of approximately two million seconds per century. So the second has been redefined – instead of being 1/86,400th part of a mean solar day, it has now been calculated as 1/31,556,925,9747th part of a solar year. I like facts – they are the bricks of reason.

It's also a fact that I woke up the next morning covered in spew. It was caked all over my chest like a plaster cast. I'd also wet myself. I mused on this and realised that my body hadn't reacted so violently to drugs for as long as I could remember. I stumbled stiffly into the bathroom. There I showered, shampooed and brushed my teeth, saving shaving until last, hoping to be awake by then. But it was not to be and I cut myself. I stared into the mirror – a pair of brand-new red lips pouted on my cheek. Quickly I kissed them with a Band-aid.

In the kitchen, as I considered breakfast, my tabby, Ken, had a few things to say to me. He was sitting hunched on top of the fridge and was especially eloquent as he hadn't been fed for twenty-four hours. I speedily opened a tin of trout and pickle flavoured Whiskas (his favourite) and gave him a double helping. Then I cheerfully blazed some toast.

Breakfast over, I became the responsible lab technician I always was in those days and scooted around the flat doing all my essential checks and chores.

An hour later, I was returning to the fifth floor, having just finished the main feed on the third floor, when Rachel, my gecko, jumped on me.

I kept quite a few geckos at that time. Rachel was tame and like Ken, had the run of the place, where she bullied the other geckos and kept the flat's unofficial cockroach collection respectful. I turned her upside down and tickled her feet. If you ever have trouble with a gecko just turn it upside down and tickle its feet. It works. Honestly! Next I did some physiotherapy.

Every day I worked for at least an hour on my phizzes. This was quite apart from the weight training I did twice a week at The Club. It was all a bit of a bore really, yet without it my joints and tendons would have quickly stiffened, so I had no choice. Although I'd fractured my spine in three places in the car crash, I was lucky, because there was minimal damage to the nerve fibres of my spinal cord. So with crutches, I could walk reasonably well. Nonetheless, I was spastic with exaggeration of the tendon reflexes at the top of my legs. But as they were nearly always covered, most of the time, my spasticity was invisible.

Things could have been a lot worse. Some of the poor bastards down at The Club were fully tetraplegic. That's adios from the neck down. At least I could piss and crap when I wanted to, which was more than they could. I skipped my sit-ups that day, but to keep my hand in did thirty extra arm presses instead.

5. Angel's Leap

Random Thoughts And Themes – priceless history. The King of Bohemia at the Battle of Crécy, because he was blind and therefore had to be led into battle by his courtiers, where he was promptly hacked into so many pieces that he was later buried in a 'small silver bucket'.

It was a hospital day. As I cruised down the driveway, I stared out across the square. Underneath the horse chestnut trees, two squirrels chased each other, skating across a mush of fermenting leaves. There was no time for messing about that morning as I had an appointment with my sister's specialist. So I topped up the chair with derv at the village's Jet garage, and taking the bridle path behind the church, tore off across the common.

I chose the round route to Southfields, which was a two-mile burn over some of the fastest dirt tracks in South London. Sometimes, late at night with fog lamps fixed to our chairs, the club boys and I would have races on the figure of eight. This was an old police motorcycle circuit and was excellent – you could approach speeds of 40mph if the surface was hard enough, which for a motorised wheelchair, on dry mud, wasn't bad.

That morning, as I sped down a nettled pathway, a fluorescent green dragonfly as big as my hand darted in front of my face. The common was itchy with insects, but as I approached the figure of eight – tragedy! I ran over a toad. I got him right across the neck too. And as the air blew back inside him, there was a neat BOK! and his belly burst. I slammed to a halt. It was a pisser, but as with the dead weasel, waste not want not, so I cut the toad's head off, sample-bagged it and sped on.

When I reached the figure of eight it was still a bit dewy. Some of the deeper dips even had puddles. Yet I did a few circuits, to get the feel of the ground, then swung up the hill to The Leap.

Angel's Leap was a mud slalom that had a vertical drop of about 15ft on its sheer side. It was intended for motorcycles and mountain bikes, though sitting at the top that morning, I stared out at the common's soft green canopy and knew I just *had* to do it.

Revving the chair hard, I slammed into first and skidded down the path. Air lashed in my face, mud grasped at the wheels and suddenly I was airborne. But as soon as I was flying I was crashing back to ground again, the front shockers smashing closed with a nasty crunching sound. Yet I'd done it! I'd jumped Angel's Leap in a wheelchair!

6. The Heath

Random Thoughts And Themes – love and losing weight. Six million human beings make love at any given moment. When they do they will each use up 200 calories at a time. Beats jogging.

Putney Heath Hospital bordered the common on its South-fields side. A busy place, it possessed a brain damage unit of a unique kind, the Persistent Vegetative State (PVS) Ward, which was, of course, why my sister was there.

On PVS, nurses and care assistants bustled. PVS at The Heath always had a positive, friendly atmosphere, I have to say that. There friends and relatives could visit at any time. Consequently, you would nearly always find at least one or two visitors, day or night.

I wheeled around a small group of patients who were sitting staring out into the hospital gardens. Most had feet and hands that had turned inwards, which is a common PVS characteristic, and all of them had their heads supported in metal braces. I paused for a moment and gazed out into the garden with them. We watched a breeze gently rock a huge elm and a thrush look for breakfast on the lawn, then I heard singing. It was a girl's voice and it was coming from Eva's room. I wheeled swiftly to her door.

'There ...' said Kim, staring hard into her brother's face, 'my birthday boy. Did you like that?'

Kim had been singing Happy Birthday to Richard, who shared the room with my sister and was a victim of iatrogenesis. While in hospital having a minor operation on his sinuses, there was a cock-up with the anaesthetic and his bloodstream was filled with bubbles of carbon monoxide.

This only lasted for a minute and fifty seconds, but it was enough for him to suffer massive brain damage. Kim took hold of Richard's head and carefully shook it from side to side and he rewarded her by grunting, though whether this was a true reaction or not, was difficult to say.

'Now,' said Kim, beaming, 'tell Dean how old you are.'

There was silence.

'Come on, Richard …'

Again silence.

'You're twenty-two, aren't you?' said Kim, a nanosecond from embarrassment. 'Twenty-two!'

'So how's the house coming on?' I said, sitting down on the bed, desperately wanting to change the subject.

'We're just waiting for the therapy pool to go in and that's that.'

'So when are you leaving?'

'The beginning of next week. Now you're going to come and visit us, aren't you, Dean? I know it's not around the corner, but Plymouth's not that far.'

'You invite me – I'll be there.'

When Kim went into Putney shopping for an hour, I turned to my sister. Someone had placed a bowl on her bedside table that was filled with huge blood-red apples so shiny they looked as if they'd been varnished. I took one of them and bit into it deeply. Eva had the bed near the window and lay, as ever, inert, with her long red hair flowing across the sheets.

Although Evangeline was not asleep, I often wondered whether she dreamed or not. Because before the accident, we would often sit and discuss our dreams. Eva's were fantastic filmic affairs that could go on for ages. I missed those chats a lot. Sometimes when I was with her and feeling this way, Eva would turn her head as if trying to sympathise. Probably coincidence, but these are images of my sister that I'll never forget – fathoms deep within herself, occasionally stirring, in a red and white sea of hair and cotton.

I gave her her feed.

I fed Evangeline whenever I visited. She never had any

lasting problems breathing and was only on a ventilator for a very brief period after the accident, but at this time, she was totally dependent and had specially prepared liquid food pumped from bottles straight into her stomach. After she'd finished her meal, as it were, I sat with her for a while.

That day I'd brought Eva a present – some new pyjamas. These were covered in appliquéd moths and butterflies. Before the accident, my sister had had lots of clothes that were made that way. Then I noticed that her toy animals had been disarranged. Along the windowsill she had a bear, a hippo, a giraffe, a snake, two rabbits, a badger and her favourite – a dolphin. I put them back in their proper order. In PVS, those sorts of things are important.

When Kim came back from Putney, we had a cup of coffee in the ground-floor coffee bar and talked about her move to Plymouth in more detail.

'Will you look after Richard all day,' I said, 'or go to work and get a carer in?'

'There's a law centre in Plymouth. I'm hoping I'll be able to do a bit of voluntary work there for an afternoon or two …'

'I've never been to Plymouth.'

'When I've got everything together, come down for a holiday.'

'Can I bring my sister?'

'Once I've got myself straight, you can bring Mum, Dad and Grandma if you like.'

'Unlikely, as Mum, Dad and Grandma are all dead, I'm afraid.'

'No problem, other people's relatives alive or dead are all the same to me.'

'You mean I could still bring them?'

'Of course … I assume they're not very noisy?'

'That's right, they're definitely on the quiet side. But they're never any trouble. Just give them a nice cool spot to lie in and you can leave them for yonks.'

'That settles it – when are you all coming down?'

After a two-year battle with her area health authority, Kim had won nearly a half a million pounds' compensation for Richard. She'd done magnificently well. Mind you, she was a lawyer, which had obviously helped. With the money she'd set up a trust for her brother, bought a house and set about having it Richardised.

Kim and I had known each other almost two and a half years, which had been difficult times, yet through it all we'd become good friends. Frankly, it was a bit more than that on my side, because I'd fallen in love with her. Yes, it was pathetic – she was the attractive, educated, mobile woman and I was the spotty, emotionally vulnerable cripple. An impossible couple. Sad but true.

7. Guttman

Random Thoughts And Themes – transport. Trains and roads are good, but if we had huge conveyor belts going up and down the country it would be better and cheaper, you could just hop on and off without any fuss or ticket-buying nonsense.

At two o'clock I went back upstairs for my interview with Doctor Guttman. Unusually, I found the door to his office open and him sat at his desk waiting for me. This immediately put me on my guard. Being so important – the Head of Aftercare, no less – Guttman was often late for his appointments and occasionally failed to turn up at all. Yet here he was waiting for *me*. Something was up, no question.

'Dean, how are you?'

'I'm well, doctor …'

He removed his glasses and we shook hands. I sat down and parked my sticks against his green leather chesterfield. There was a subtle protest in his eyes at this, but I ignored it.

'I've been seeing quite a few relatives of patients in the PVS Ward lately,' he said, leaning back in his chair. 'You know the whole PVS issue is causing great controversy at the moment …'

He was being relaxed and chatty – again it was a bad sign, because he was setting me up for something.

'Six months ago, at a special conference, a PVS think-tank was set up and it has just reported back. What we needed were agreed guidelines …'

'You need guidelines, doctor, I need my sister. I hope there's some common ground.'

Guttman laughed. A tight, over-quickly sort of laugh.

'How are your studies going, by the way? You are at?'

'I'm not at anywhere at the moment, although I'm due to start at Surrey soon.'

'Studying?'

'Microbiology.'

We stared at each other. I wasn't giving him the moisture from my dioxide exhalation and he knew it. He suddenly frowned. Here it comes, I thought.

'Dean, there is a growing consensus that patients who have no meaningful existence and will never recover should not be kept alive indefinitely.'

Again he paused and stared at me. He was looking for a hint of understanding, complicity, anything, but again I gave him nothing. You're going solo with this one, Guttman, I thought.

'Another issue is whether scarce resources should be spent on patients who cannot reap the benefit of those resources. The patient who is diagnosed as PVS has no self-regarding interests. So in some cases, there seems to be no reason to continue life-sustaining treatments ...'

Here he took up Eva's records and wagged them at me.

'Now Dean, Evangeline is in that category. Her higher brain has more space than I would like. Three separate neurologists have agreed that she has no prospects of recovery. And this conclusion has come after some of the most exhaustive neurological tests ever performed at this hospital.'

He leaned forward, but his tone softened.

'It's been two years and there's nothing. She's gone, my boy. She's just not there any more ...'

'Just hold it right there!' I said, I was shaking, 'I think you've just made an equation between life and money, but it's not the place of a doctor or group of doctors, no matter how important, to decide on the lives of hundreds of PVS patients around the world. It's the community that must decide. This is not a medical issue. It's a matter of simple humanity!'

I was blazing. It had been two years, yes, two years of nothing but disappointment. Yet all at once Eva's white face was before me, her smiling, loving face and suddenly I felt a great surge of confidence roll inside me.

'You say – let her go, but she 's my sister. She's all I have and she is *there*, I know it. You either care for her here, doctor, or I'll take her home with me and look after her there. I'm over eighteen and her next of kin, so I can do it. Don't think for one moment that any accountant, lawyer or committee of doctors will bamboozle me out of my rights, or my sister out of hers. The decision is not yours, Doctor Guttman, it's mine. Because I made up my mind a long time ago that I would be there for my sister. And she will live!'

What could he say? Not much and he knew it. I just wondered how many relatives had fallen for the tosser's ethics and balance sheet. Or perhaps he was testing the whole thing out on me, I don't know. Oddly enough this was not the first time doctors had told me that Eva was finished. When I saw her for the first time after the accident, she was covered in scabs and bruises and had tubes coming out everywhere. They said then that her brain damage was so severe that she would not live more than a few days. Yet two weeks later, she was out of intensive care and having her first physiotherapy. If this accident has taught me anything positive, it's that finally, in everything you do, you must follow your instincts. And those that seek to guide you, who have any self-interest whatsoever, must be either watched carefully, or, if they get tricksy, fought to a standstill. There's no other way.

8. Michael's

Random Thoughts And Themes – things that move fast. Cars. Trains. Aircraft. Spacecraft. Wind. Fire. Bad news. The jet stream. A running dog. A wasp flying at full tilt. My hand when wanking.

On the way home from the hospital, I made a detour to the village pet shop. It was a few doors down from the Double Bubble and was actually run by Maurice's brother, Michael. Physically the two men were very alike, even to the extent of their pot bellies, yet they could not have been more unlike in temperament. While Maurice was genial and only a clinical depressive on occasion, Michael was proudly sour and monosyllabic all of the time. I pushed at the door, an old-fashioned shop bell ting-a-linged above my head and a warm stench of animal urine hit me hard in the nose.

'Now, Michael, how are you?'

He was sitting behind the counter holding a salamander in one hand and a lizard in the other.

'All right, I suppose,' he said, quietly.

At that moment, a peach-cheeked lovebird gave a loud, piercing cry and then a cage full of puppies broke into frantic yapping.

'So what's new?' I said.

'Nothing.'

'Nothing?'

'No.'

'Well, what are you doing with those two?' I said, gesturing at the salamander and the lizard.

His cheeks coloured slightly.

'Just checking stock.'

Trying to decide which was which, more like, I thought, as I stepped closer.

'Ah, a Skett's salamander and a Colombian corn lizard. You must have had a delivery from South America?'

'This morning.'

'Any wolf spiders? I'm looking for a replacement due to an untimely bereavement.'

Just then the salamander leapt from Michael's grasp, scampered across the counter and threw itself on top of a mynah bird's cage. The mynah immediately screamed, which set the whole shop off – parrots, lovebirds, canaries, covey doves, kittens, puppies, even the frogs screeched, howled and yowled.

I made a grab for the salamander. But he saw me coming and dived through the bars of a cage of cottontail rabbits then sprang straight back out, though I soon cornered him at the bottom of a parrakeet's aviary.

'Thanks a lot,' said Michael, taking the salamander back. 'No, I haven't any wolf spiders, but I can order some.'

'If you would,' I said, 'and I need some locusts.'

'How many?'

'Give me six boxes.'

A few minutes later, I called into the Double Bubble to play some pinball, but it was late afternoon and the machines were all taken by schoolchildren.

'Maurice,' I said, leaning on the counter, 'what was Michael like as a boy?'

Maurice was frying pieces of bacon, which hissed and sizzled across the griddle in the shape of a great red and white question mark.

'Just the same as he is now – a miserable devil. I remember Dad offering him a sixpence to smile once, but Michael wouldn't do it. That's the truth.'

'Come on …' I said.

'No, as I stand here, it's true.'

I sat down with a cup of tea and a custard tart, but I was still buzzing with the row with Guttman, so when Maurice for a moment joined me, I sounded him out.

'Guttman wants to pull the plug on Eva,' I said, 'he thinks she's too expensive. Talk about depressing …'

'That seems to be the shape of things in healthcare nowadays,' said Maurice, 'everyone's under pressure to pay their way.'

I smacked the custard tart hard with my fork, which promptly split the pastry in half.

'But it's all so obscene, it's as if they want to throw out the most expensive patients, to save money. What happened to Putney Heath being the leader in PVS research?'

'It does seem unfair. Unless this really is a complete ethical rethink.'

I split the tart into three parts with another blow.

'I come back to the same equation again and again – how can people be left to suffer for the lack of money? A trauma is a trauma and should be dealt with as such, not used as some sort of financial manoeuvre.'

'Are you actually going to eat that tart?'

I stared down at the shattered cake.

'No. I'm going to look after it. I'm going to give it medication access, plenty of alternative and mainstream therapy; I'm going to stick by this pastry through thick and thin …'

As I was returning to Witley a wind blew that was so cold it hurt my face. And as I rounded the corner of Bessborough Road, I passed a gaggle of Ashburton Boys.

The Ashburton Boys were a drug gang originally from an area near Putney called the Ashburton Estate. Vile had had a couple of run-ins with the AB's over various deals and now refused to have anything to do with them. But they would not go away, mainly because the drug scene in Roehampton was worth so much money.

'Hey, look who it is,' said one of them, 'that cunt with the wheels for legs.'

They laughed. I said nothing, as always.

9. The Menagerie

Random Thoughts And Themes – things that move slowly. Stones. Parked cars. Hot weather. Anything micro scale (relatively speaking). A hardened heart.

I woke on the Saturday morning to find Rachel sitting on top of my head. She'd brought me a present – half a mouse. I looked at the alarm clock – 7am. That's the trouble with animals – a lie-in is a concept they never quite understand. I turned over, determined to try and sleep for at least another half an hour, when a commotion broke out on the Bird and Mammal Floor.

I've never been very keen on keeping wild birds in cages, but they were vital to The Happy Room, so I had no choice. In those days I kept over a dozen birds of prey, so things could get quite noisy on the fourth floor. The hoo-ha was centred around two honey buzzards. So I fed them and they quietened down. Then, as I was up, I decided that I might as well feed the rest of the birds, but the intercom buzzed.

'JC calling,' said a voice.

'JC?' I said.

'Jesus Christ, the Son of Man, who else? I wonder if you could spare me a few minutes. I've some vital information to impart?'

This happened all the time on the estate, you were forever being bothered by every kind of knocker-pest and God-junky. I tried to be polite, but it was a strain at times, particularly at 7am in the morning.

'Er, now look, Mr Christ, it's a bit early for callers, wouldn't you say?'

'God's work is a 24 hour project, besides, I'm the night shift, I'm just finishing.'

'You're the night shift!?!'

'The Lord is my king and shepherd and I go where he bids me to go and *when*.'

I hung up. A God-junky doing a night-shift – how he wasn't arrested or seriously injured was baffling. Quickly, I finished feeding all the birds and then called down to the fish and insects' floor.

One of my very first animal interests was insects. Mainly because they were cheap and easy to keep. I was especially fascinated by spiders. And it wasn't long before I had a reasonable collection, which included – bird-eating spiders, wolf spiders, jumping spiders, a pair of black widows and a wonderfully poisonous Sydney funnel-web.

One disadvantage of keeping insects is that many suffer very short lifespans, which can sometimes consist of only a few weeks. Longevity is, generally speaking, swopped for high activity rates. But I did possess a magnificent common house spider, *Ternaries domestica*, that lived to the grand old age of four years. Which in our terms is nearly three hundred years old!

After feeding the insects, I began on the fish.

If insects are fascinating, then fish are utterly mesmerising. Because again, most fish are easy to keep and their behaviour patterns are anything but dull. I kept hundreds of different species in about ten separate tanks, most of which were salt water aquaria. These included bass, houting, salmon, sturgeon, and my treasure of the deep – Julie, a six-foot conger eel.

I'd grown Julie from fry. She'd been with me for nearly five years and as a result was so affectionate she'd eat from my hand. Now conger eels have a reputation for violence that goes before them somewhat. Indeed, Julie had a mouthful of teeth that at full stretch was over a foot in diameter, but she was a very gentle fish and also clever. Although I didn't understand just how clever until I had a problem with fish going missing.

It was about a year after the accident, somehow I was losing fish from the third floor, often as many as ten a day. As I've just said, I kept a large stock – over five hundred individuals – so at first, I didn't notice that anything was wrong. But gradually, I began to realise that someone, or something, was raiding the nursery tanks.

I suspected Ken and virtually every other animal that I had and even laid traps, placing little alarms around the tanks. Now this went on for about three weeks and I was getting a bit desperate, when late one night, I went down to the Fish Room to look for a writing pad I'd mislaid and couldn't believe what I saw, for Julie was hanging half out of her tank and half out of another, gorging herself on young zebra fish.

I made a secure lid for her tank there and then. Which she wasn't too happy about, but it had to be done. She was my favourite fish, yet at that rate, would have eaten almost my entire marine and tropical collection inside a month.

The phone rang. I looked at my watch. It was still not 7.30am.

'This is Jesus again …'

'WHERE DID YOU GET MY PHONE NUMBER FROM!?!' I bellowed.

'The Lord has provided …'

'If you don't ring off, I'll call the police.'

'I just want to talk to you.'

'You're wasting your time. I'm a genetics evolutionist – great omnipotent exterior forces mean nothing to me.'

'The Lord can help anyone, no matter how lost …'

I slammed the phone down. Ken, who was sitting on top of the fridge, gave me a why-are-you-getting-so-worked-up look. But there's nothing like a bit of old-style lose-your-rag anger now and again. It's good for the psyche.

After I'd washed, dressed and had a slice of toast, I went down to the second floor and had a look at another problem – my king cobra.

If I had to choose from all my specimens, I think my honest to God, never to be topped favourites would be my snakes. There's just something about them. They are absolutely beautiful.

The king was tightly coiled in a corner of his tank. I was worried, as in the three weeks that I'd had him, he hadn't eaten a thing. Snakes can go for quite lengthy periods without eating, but this had gone on too long. Paradoxically, some of the deadliest creatures in the wild are the most timid and prissy in captivity. So I dangled a dead field mouse from the top of the tank, but the king wouldn't budge. Then, as I stared at him, I had an idea. I took the dead mouse through to the second-floor kitchen and carefully skinned it. In the wild, prey always has a distinct scent, which in captivity is difficult to duplicate. Having skinned the mouse, I covered it in chicken blood and then went back and again lowered it into the tank. This time the snake stirred and sleepily opened his eyes. I grinned. He was hungry after all.

10. Hammy

Random Thoughts And Themes – things that over the years have lost their power. The family. Teachers. White chocolate. The English Breakfast. Bass guitarists. String vests.

I started collecting animals at the age of six. My very first creature was a striped hamster which was given to me by my Aunt June on my sixth birthday. I called him Hammy after a character in a sixties TV series my mother told me about and quickly became besotted.

The cage was fun too – shiny blue, chrome bars with a tiny treadmill in one corner. Well, I played with Hammy all day and dreamed about him all night. These were funny, odd dreams where I'd be floating across fields with my mouth stuffed with leaves, or riding naked on the back of something huge and warm.

About two months after Hammy arrived I came home from school one day to find his cage empty. My mother and I pulled the flat apart. Cupboards. Wardrobes. Dressers. We went out on to the landing and pulled that apart too. We searched for hours, but found nothing. Somehow Hammy had completely disappeared. It was all deeply traumatic.

It took a while. Months. But eventually I forgot about Hammy. Although during the early part of this time, if anyone was foolish enough to mention his name, I'd instantly become catatonic with grief. Looking back it must have been almost a year after the hamster's disappearance, when we threw out our old sofa. My mother was given this particular sofa by her mother, who got it from my great-grandmother. Needless to say, the sofa was well past its best mother. So after a new sofa was delivered, the old three-mother one was parked on the landing and the next day carried to the estate dump by two caretakers.

The dump was at the back of the boiler house and was one of my favourite places. I would go there to play secretly with forbidden things like nails and broken glass. There thrown-away bits and pieces took on other lives – bicycle forks became double-ended spears; spent bulbs – bombs; lengths of chain – fierce whips.

It looked weird, our old three-seater balanced on a pile of coke. When the caretakers had gone, I picked up a rusty iron railing and began to smash the sofa with it. Dust stormed and wood cracked. I ripped the upholstery right down to the bare frame. Then something caught my eye – a small, white, furry disc trapped between a spring. I eased it out. It was Hammy. Little Hammy hamster, quite dead and flat as a 50p piece. I don't know how it happened, but the hamster had escaped into the sofa, got tangled in a spring and was squashed when someone sat down on it. I stared hard at him. Hammy was so flat he looked like a cigarette card. So that's what he became, as I flipped and flicked him all over the estate.

11. Those Chairs

Random Thoughts And Themes – romantic insects. The Venus moth, because the male mates and then dies. He pops his clogs because he doesn't have a penis. Instead, when he mates he disengages his entire stomach, so eventually dies of starvation.

That second Saturday of September was warm and for the time of year still fairly bright. In the evening, along Bessborough Road, I saw some children playing by a crab apple tree. One of them threw a stick up into the tree's branches and to their delighted screams, a cluster of the bitter little apples sprayed down into the road.

There was a small group of paraplegics in Roehampton, including me, who scoffed at our Roehampton Rehab Centre and all that it stood for. Yet there was one thing good about it – it possessed some excellent sports equipment, especially for weight training.

As I arrived that evening a medicine ball flew through the doorway. Instinctively, I dropped my sticks, caught the ball and fell to the ground.

'Here he is,' said Four-wheel-drive, poking his head around the doorway. 'Witley Man …'

'Know what they'll put in Witley's place after they've levelled it,' said Ishmael.

'A DSS cybernetics plant?' I said, pulling myself to my feet.

'No, a sports centre for the able-bodied.'

'Sad,' we chimed in unison.

Inside the gym, as I yanked my tracksuit on, Ishmael pitched his chair onto one wheel and for a full thirty seconds held himself in perfect balance.

'Straight …' said Ishmael, eventually banging the wheel to the ground, 'what are you going to do if they tear Witley down?'

'It won't come to that,' I said.

'But the council are going to court.'

'Well, tomorrow they're going to try and agree on whether
 they should go to court or not.'

'If they do that's it.'

'They'll never evict us from Witley, Ish. Because they've no
 real idea what they're up against.'

Four-wheel-drive was swinging back and forth on a rope. At a height of 12ft, he suddenly let go and smashed back into the seat of his wheelchair.

'Okay, let's go,' he said.

We warmed up with a circuit, which took about ten minutes, then we moved over to the bench presses. You can develop muscle stamina with expanders, spring-grips and bar-bells and weightlifters use them. But a truly effi-cient muscle builder is a bench press, for if used properly it exercises all the muscles that count in weightlifting and exercises them together, so you get an even development. At that time, I'd only been weightlifting for a few months and was classed as a lightweight. Actually, I wasn't weightlifting, I was power-lifting, which has different tech-niques. But what was really good was that Ishmael and Four-wheel-drive were both former UK Para Weightlifting Champions, so I got the best tuition I could have wished for.

'I tell you what,' said Ishmael, lifting a 150lb bar a clear 4ft, 'if they do fuck over Witley, it'll be Danebury Avenue next.'

'That's what I say,' said Four-wheel-drive, pumping a 70lb frame at speed with one arm.

'I doubt that,' I said, struggling to hold up a 70lb frame with both arms. 'Danebury hasn't been up ten years. But if you're worried, come down to the town hall tomorrow.'

Four-wheel-drive halted in mid-pump. 'Have they got a canteen?'

'It's a town hall,' said Ishmael, 'not a motorway caff.'

'Not that I know of,' I said. 'You could always take a flask, though.'

'And a pack-up?'

'I don't see why not.'

We trained for about an hour then Bim and Lucy arrived.

A small part of the rehab centre was an engineering bay, where all kinds of day and evening classes took place. Here, I had my own bench for my chair-engineering. I lined up five mugs.

'Remember, five sugars,' said Four-wheel-drive.

'Your teeth are going to dissolve, do you know that?' I said.

'No legs, no teeth. I could cope.'

Lucy sniggered, which made Four-wheel-drive curl with pleasure. He fancied Lucy badly – a fact which Ishmael and I often tormented him with.

'Right, who's first?' I said.

'Could you have a look at my chain?' said Lucy, 'it keeps slipping.'

Carefully, she got out of her chair and we pushed it onto its side.

The first petrol-driven 'invalid carriage' took to the pavements in 1899. Self-propelled wheelchairs from then on were nearly always driven by electricity. Now electricity is an ecological, cost-effective way of motorising a wheelchair and the electric wheelchairs you can buy today are well made and reliable. The problem is that their top speed is never more than about 15mph. I remember sitting in one once and being overtaken by a poodle on a lead. Shame energised me. So I took an Everest Jennings wheelchair frame, a 50cc Honda moped engine and put the two together. Surprizingly, it worked quite well. The transmission was chain driven, with twin wheels either side, balanced by the usual two swivel wheels at the front. My first conversions were rough and ready, though, and I had quite a few spills to start with. Yet gradually, I managed to iron out the major mechanical problems, which centred around torque and the efficiency of the chain drive.

'Try that,' I said, having shortened the chain.

I pushed the wheelchair back onto its wheels and Lucy climbed back into it. She started the engine and swung out through the big bay doors across the basketball pitch. We watched her for a while, crashing through the gears, and then Ishmael and I began to strip the plugs from Bim's chair, as it was due a service.

While we did this we parked Bim on one of the benches. Bim was a full tetraplegic and also dumb. Yet he was always playing tricks and making jokes, which when you're paralysed from the neck down and dumb to boot, takes some doing. But he managed it in some fiendishly clever ways. For example, that evening, while sitting on the bench he began to whistle. This was a sound that we'd never heard him make before.

'Bim's whistling,' said Four-wheel-drive.

'So?' said Ishmael.

'He's whistling – God Save The Queen.'

It was true. I turned and stared into Bim's creamy-white, smiling face. Yet for the life of me I couldn't work it out.

'He means that *this is royal*,' said Four-wheel-drive.

'What do you mean *this is royal*?' said Ishmael.

'That it's good, that he likes it.'

'Likes what?'

'Likes *this*, what we're doing, *us* …'

'But maybe he just likes the tune,' I said.

There was one major disadvantage with my motorised wheelchairs and that was the gearbox. Because the engines had to do a fair bit of pulling, I had to low-ratio the gearboxes. Unfortunately, they were not designed for that sort of abuse, so they would occasionally fail. But I was working on it. One possibility was to run another carburettor in series, which would put the fuel consumption up, yet give extra acceleration, meaning less wear and tear on the gearbox. Another was simply to rebuild the gearboxes to specification, which was the best, but also the most expensive solution. At that moment, Lucy tore back into the bay. It was then that I noticed that her chair's exhaust had an unusually throaty murmur.

'Better?' I said.

'Much,' said Lucy, 'it didn't slip once.'

Clouds of blue smoke were billowing from her chair's exhaust.

'Turn off your engine, please,' I said.

Lucy climbed out of the chair once more and we turned it onto its side again and found a gaping gash in the silencer box. But it wasn't a worn hole. It had been cut. Someone had actually taken a hacksaw to it.

'Know anything about this?' I said, pointing to the damaged
 silencer.

'No, nothing,' said Lucy.

Ishmael sank to his knees and ran a finger along the jagged tear of the hole.

'Where do you keep the chair at night?' he said.

'Sometimes I have to leave it outside. I haven't got a shed and it won't fit in the hallway.'

'Well, it looks as if someone's been fiddling with it,' I said.

'Really?'

This was par for the course, as we'd been seeing little acts of vandalism on wheelchairs all over Roehampton for months. Even Ishmael had had his chair's seat slashed one night outside the library. I unhooked the gas welder and took a metal plate from the scrap bin.

'Hold on a second,' said Four-wheel-drive.

In one go, he grabbed Lucy's chair and lifted it onto the tackle hook. This was a dead-weight of at least 13 stone. Lucy looked away. Ishmael and I grinned.

'You know, Four, one day you'll be able to grow a wheelchair,' I said, lighting the welder.

'Honestly?' he said.

'Did you ever grow crystals in a glass of water?'

'Yeah, once, at Christmas. They came out of a cracker.'

I explained that some recent research into the molecular structure of metals was based on a study of animal teeth and sea shells. For teeth and sea shells are not only very strong and durable but have been grown. In other words, they possess a molecular structure that has reacted to a shape-changing program. So if you could understand, from a molecular perspective, how teeth and sea shells react to shape-changing, in theory, you could apply that knowledge to any material. Even metal. Because all you're really talking about is molecular structural control. Therefore in the future, it may be possible to grow things from virtually anything. You would simply program the material to change shape and a sheet of aluminium would become a car door, or an electric kettle, whatever.

'A CD player,' said Four-wheel-drive, 'I'd grow a CD player.'

Suddenly there was the sound of smashing glass as the panels of the workshop doors disintegrated. I doused the gas welder and Ishmael and Four-wheel-drive hopped across to the doors. Someone had slotted a length of scaffolding through the handles from the outside. Four-wheel leaned his bulk against the doors and with a crack the frames shattered like balsawood. He stared out into the freezing night, his breath instantaneously vaporising.

'Let the fuckers come ...' he said, 'let them come!'

12. Two Pints of Lager
and a Packet of Crisps, Please

Random Thoughts And Themes – things that are spectacular. Photosynthesis. A blue whale giving birth. A scorpion fly giving birth. Three hotels on Mayfair.

By the time we'd cleared everything up and made the centre secure again, it was getting on for ten o'clock, but we still went down to the Montague. Where I had one or two drinks more than usual, which was not like me. In fact I had five pints in less than forty minutes, which was unheard of for me. Then as I sat staring at Lucy, who was chatting to Four-wheel-drive, it struck me what it was about a girl I really liked. It was the mouth. Yes, there was definitely something special about a nicely shaped, full mouth. And then a verse came to me –

> every morning
> padding noiselessly
> he would carefully collect her mouth
> from its hiding place
> gently tilt it to his lips
> and greedily taste her

It was way past midnight when I got home. And when I finally managed to open the door of the flat, I found Ken and Rachel waiting up for me. It was rather comical, as they were sitting side by side on top of the broken fridge-freezer. This cosy all-pals-together act was something new. I sat down beside them and as Ken stepped down into my lap, all at once I felt dead sober and began to think of Francesca.

Francesca was my first real girlfriend. Real is the right word here, because I had sex with her. Well, actually I didn't have sex with her, but it was close.

Before the accident, I was a keen walker and so I thought was Francesca. So that's what we did – went walking everywhere, in Oxfordshire, Cambridgeshire, Kent, Sussex and planned a trip to Scotland. But as it later turned out, she wasn't enthusiastic about our walking at all and had just been trying to please me.

The crunch came when we were out one Sunday, near a place called Steyning, in Sussex. It was late autumn, wet and windy. We'd mapped out a route that would swing us in a 10 mile circle, past a manor house, an ancient bridge and alongside a river. A pleasant, medium-length Sunday afternoon walk. Though I could sense things were not quite right with Francesca, for when we were only a mile out, she was irritably puffing and blowing all over the place. Then it began to rain. A very fine drizzle-veil. The sort of rain that gets in everywhere. Soon, even though we were wearing cagoules, we were wet through. Suddenly a bramble stem caught at Francesca's throat and dragged her to the ground. She just sat there in the mud, her neck streaked red.

'I don't want to do this,' she said. 'I don't want to do this!'

I looked at her neck – the red was only blackberry juice. But she wouldn't go any further. And looking back, I don't blame her. I should have been more attentive and considerate. I should have realised that in going walking with me, she was just being nice. But I didn't. Life is a bramble stem. Grasp it and cry.

I gave Ken and Rachel some supper, which was the real reason they were waiting up for me and then went down to the second floor. I had a pregnant sea horse I was keeping an eye on.

It is the male sea horse that gives birth, as the female, after fertilization, transfers the eggs into the male's stomach pouch. A pouch, incidentally, complete with placental fluids. But you have to watch things, as when the young are born, given the chance, the male will not hesitate to eat them.

In the large nursery tank, the expectant father drifted motionless as if held by invisible threads. He'd been like that for weeks. So much so that it was beginning to cross my mind that either he wasn't pregnant after all, or he'd already given birth and eaten the lot.

While I was there, I switched on the fluorescent of the conger's tank and immediately Julie slid from a rocky hole, finned a crab aside, who wasn't moving fast enough, and snaked to the surface. I put my hand into the water and the huge eel slid underneath it, rolling her body with pleasure as she did so.

Eels have very thin skins, so they can almost certainly feel a touch as well as any human. Usually, I would bring a titbit for her, but that evening I'd forgotten. I looked around for something and my eye fell on the pregnant sea horse. No, I thought, I can't. Then I heard an ugly screaming sound coming from the bird and mammal floor.

It was the honey buzzards again. I had serious doubts that this pair were ever going to mate. They just didn't seem to like one other. The female certainly had reservations about the male. And this was a surprise because he was quite a suave specimen. It was something I thought I might let The Happy Room sort out, but so everyone could get some sleep, I put the female in a separate aviary and moved her into the kitchen. Then I went to the bathroom, dropped my jeans and sat down on the toilet seat. It was past 1am and very quiet. A lorry passing by outside was suddenly loud, but turned and faded into the night and then it became extremely quiet. So quiet, in fact, that I found myself listening to my breathing and a funny little sticking and unsticking sound coming from deep inside my chest. Before I could investigate further I laid an enormous turd into the bowl. No warning. No mercy. I looked down at it. Sure enough, it was a monster and possessed, rather curiously, a slender taper at one end. Odd. Very odd, I thought to myself. I began to hum. I don't know why. I never normally hum.

13. Committed and Steadfast

Random Thoughts And Themes – SAS insects. The yellow dung fly, because it can mount an insect as large as itself, pierce it with its armoured proboscis, and suck the fluids dry within 60 seconds.

Next morning, on my way out, I bumped into Webley. Webley was the Witley and Hilsea caretaker and someone I avoided whenever possible. Which this morning proved impossible. Predictably, as soon as he saw me the old bastard launched into a tirade about my wheelchair.

'It's not allowed,' he said.

'Yes, but where else can I put it?'

'You've got a shed, put it in there.'

'It's damp and unsafe.'

'Well, you can't keep leaving it here …'

As he continued, I started the chair and revved the accelerator hard. The din drowned the caretaker's voice and as the twin exhausts began to purr I let out the clutch and suddenly swerved out of the building, leaving him standing in a fog of black smoke.

Caretakers don't get much of a good press, do they? And this is down to the job mostly, as they're dead-end jobs. To top that, many caretakers have some sort of disability, so they have my sympathy there. Though I have met cheerful and helpful caretakers. The rehab centre had one. So did the town hall in Putney. But what really irritated everyone about Webley, was that as a caretaker, he was about as much use as a legless table, particularly in his first-line maintance, which was zero and as to his late night patrols – in the nineteen years that I'd been resident on the Alton Estate I'd never once seen him patrol the blocks. Lenny, who lived on the second floor of Witley, had been at war with him for years. This had caught on around the estate and as a result Webley had become a deeply unpopular figure. Once someone threw a TV at him from the eighth floor of one of the towers. He was lucky he wasn't killed. Furious, he called the police. But they refused to come. They loathed him as much as we did.

On the common that morning, I hopped through pools of marsh mud. It had been raining all night, so everything was dripping. By the stream I noticed some basil nudging some blue-eyed Mary, so I took a few handfuls of each, as my Brazilian grasshoppers loved sweet grass.

Again the traps were full and I had two surprises. One was a baby hedgehog and the other a bat! Yes, after nearly a year of trying, I'd finally caught one. She was tiny and very lousy, but otherwise in good condition. I didn't quite know what to do with the hedgehog, as he was of little interest to me as a species, but he wouldn't survive on the common, since he was not yet weaned, so I was forced to take him.

Back in the flat, as I sorted out the bat and the hedgehog, the phone rang. It was Hillary.

'What time does the meeting start?' she asked.

'6.30pm'

'Are we all going up together, or what?'

'See you there if you like.'

'Okay.'

But as I put the phone down it rang again.

'Ready for tonight then?' said Lenny.

'Of course.'

'Do you want me to bring you a sword?'

'No thanks, Len. I can manage …'

After lunch, I deloused the bat. I estimated that she was probably about six weeks old. Which was younger than I would have liked, but you can't pick and choose when you trap. When I'd finished with the bat, I deloused the baby hedgehog.

You have to be careful with delousing animals from the wild, as fleas provide a necessary stimulation of their skin and clean-ups of this kind are rarely popular with the recipients. It was just so with the hedge, as he cried rather pathetically all the way through his bath. This strange sound was enough to attract the attention of Ken and Rachel.

Ken sat by the bath bowl and was plainly amused. But Rachel was more deeply affected and at one stage actually tried to get into the bowl with the hedgehog. This served to traumatise the hedge even more, as he'd plainly never seen anything like a gecko before. Yet within minutes, he was happily scoffing some baked beans and minced meat and within half an hour, was rushing around poking his nose into everything. Though later I heard his piercing scream and found him in the kitchen, hiding behind the fridge, shaking with fright. Someone had given him a nasty stab in the nose. There was only one other animal in the room – a peregrine falcon, sitting in her cage in the corner, looking very cool and uninvolved.

The hedgehog was lucky the peregrine was off-colour with an eye infection, otherwise he'd have been dragged into the cage and shredded in seconds. It gave him his name, though. Nose. He even turned his head and blinked when I called him by it. Which was, come to think of it, the only time I can remember him paying any attention to anything I said, in the whole of his very long (for a hedgehog) life.

14. Committed We Stand

Random Thoughts And Themes – weather that I love. Thunder that's so loud it shakes the house. Very fine rain that is a mist of water. Waking up in the morning to find it's silent outside because everything's covered in that freezing cold white stuff.

At the town hall the housing committee were convening in the main council chamber, obviously expecting a crowd. And they were right to do so, for when I got there, the chamber was chock-a-block. There were councillors from every ward in the borough, press, local radio, even a TV crew. When I saw Four-wheel-drive and Lucy sitting at the back of the room I smiled and gave them a wave. There's nothing like a few wheelchairs in a confined space, to provoke genuine chaos.

'Did you bring your sandwiches!' I shouted.

'Nah, but I've got a flask!' yelled Four-wheel-drive, grinning.

He waved a yellow thermos at me. Then a reporter from the *Wandsworth Borough News* tapped me on the arm.

'Do you live on the Alton Estate?'

The man was wearing a dog-shaped earring in one ear.

'Yes,' I said, 'and have done all my life.'

'What will your reaction be if the committee votes to go for eviction orders?'

'I'll do what I've done throughout – maintain that the Alton Estate has years of life left in it yet and that come what may, we'll never be evicted.'

'Can you fight bulldozers?' The earring's tail wagged.

'Bulldozers are manned by men and if they come to the

estate we'll appeal to their sense of justice. Is it fair that people should have their homes pulled down around their ears? That's the question we'll be asking.'

'But the blocks are derelict, aren't they?'

'Not quite.'

'How many tenants are left in yours?'

'Six.'

The earring's mouth fell open. Just then the chairman of the committee, Councillor Barnes-Turner, stood up and the noise in the room fell to a murmur.

'Is the deaf signer here for Councillor Woodward?' said Barnes-Turner.

A woman stepped forward from the crowd.

'Yes, I'm sorry,' said the signer, 'I would have spoken up earlier, but I wasn't sure whether I was at the right meeting.'

'Councillor Woodward is that lady sitting at the end of the table,' said Barnes-Turner.

The signer followed Barnes-Turner's finger and then began swinging her arms back and forth in a greeting to the deaf councillor.

'Now, the room is very full,' continued the chairman, 'so I would ask people to stay calmly in their places. May I also remind everyone that this meeting does not have a public forum. In other words, the only people that can speak and vote tonight are members of the committee. I hope that's clear … Can I now draw the committee's attention to the agenda. Item one: that a court order should be acquired to evict persons known and unknown from Hilsea Tower, Dunhill Tower and Witley Tower, Alton Estate, Roehampton.'

Instantly a gaggle of girls at the back of the room screamed 'NO!!' And a scuffle broke out.

'Now I warn you all,' continued Barnes-Turner, 'that if there's any rowdiness here tonight, I will not hesitate to call the police and have the room cleared.'

'Oh yes, councillor,' said a man's voice from near the doorway, 'you'd like nothing better than to do everything in secret.'

This cued a mishmash of mutterings, but Barnes-Turner

wasn't put off, he barely paused in his stride.

'Now what I would like to do now is refer the committee to Mr Maddox, the Chief Planning Officer.'

'The position is this ...' said Maddox, nervously clearing his throat, 'the demolition of the said buildings on the Alton Estate has been agreed by this committee, the full council, and ratified by the Department of the Environment. But because the contractors were unable to begin the work on Monday the 3rd of last month, the council is in receipt of substantial abeyance costings.'

There were cries of SHAME! Which quickly began to rock the room. Barnes-Turner rose to his feet once more –

'THIS IS A FINAL WARNING. IF ORDER IS NOT RESUMED IMMEDIATELY, I'LL CALL THE POLICE, I PROMISE YOU!!'

'CALL 'EM THEN,' shouted a voice, 'IT'S ABOUT TIME WE HAD THE LAW IN 'ERE!'

There was laughter. Even Barnes-Turner smiled, but after a pause he sat down and Maddox continued –

'We've tried all channels, but the only way forward is to apply for eviction orders. Failing this, the entire Alton Park Project will be delayed again, once more leaving the council with tens of thousands of pounds in abeyance charges.'

'So,' said Barnes-Turner, cutting in, 'can I ask for this motion to be seconded, please?'

'Seconded,' said a voice from around the table.

Again the crowd began to shout – 'OUT! OUT! OUT! OUT! OUT!'

'A vote please,' shouted the chairman, over the clamour, 'ALL IN FAVOUR OF THE MOTION, PLEASE RAISE A HAND!'

Nine hands flicked into the air from the committee's twelve councillors.

'I HEREBY DECLARE ITEM ONE OF THE AGENDA PASSED!' cried Barnes-Turner.

'FIX! FIX! FIX!' screamed the room.

At that moment, from the back of the chamber, a yellow thermos, with the grim efficiency of a smart bomb, arced slowly through the air, found its target and the committee chairman hit the floor completely unconscious. Then a melee quickly became mayhem.

Police later made nine arrests and several ambulances took eleven people to hospital with various injuries.

Back on the estate oily white clouds slewed to and fro across a grey night sky. In the foyer of Witley, Lenny, Hillary, Mrs Dear and I reran the evening's events over and over.

'That flask …' said Hillary.

We tittered.

'His face …' said Mrs Dear.

We roared.

Not until we'd relived every pinch, punch and kick up the arse several times did we say goodnight.

'Fancy a beer?' said Lenny, as we were getting into the lift.

'If you like,' I said.

Lenny, in his twenties, was a schizophrenic, lived alone on the second floor and looked distinctly weird. For while inhaling helium from a plastic bag at a party, it ignited, the bag wrapped around his head and burned most of his face off. As a result, after much surgery, the skin of his face now swept from his neck in several great swerves of scarring and vortexed into a fleshy whirlpool that was his mouth, leaving slits for eyes and a small bump for a nose.

So the first time you saw Lenny, it was a bit of a shock. Moreover, as many of his face muscles had been destroyed, he had few facial expressions, so his manner took a bit of getting used to.

'What are you having?' said Lenny, opening the fridge door and gazing inside. For a moment his face, lit only by the fridge light, glowed even more grotesquely than usual.

'I've got Heineken or Holst …'

'I'll have a Holst,' I said, sitting down by the kitchen window.

Lenny handed me the can.

'Are you hungry?'

'Starving,' I said. 'I haven't eaten since breakfast.'

'Well, I haven't much except a few dates.'

From the back of the fridge Lenny took out a dish of dates that was surrounded by a thick cloud of mould.

'Tell me,' I said, 'what's the most disgusting thing you've ever offered anyone?'

But Lenny didn't reply. Instead he pulled a photo album from a drawer, wiped some grime from the cover and showed me a black and white photo of a woman cuddling a small white poodle. I gawked at a picture of a film star. She even smiled like a film star, with lots of impossibly white teeth.

'I went to stay with her when my parents split up,' said Lenny. 'She lived in Devon, on a farm. She'd come into my room late at night and suck me off.'

'She abused you?'

'Yeah.'

'That's terrible, Len. Hold on, how old were you?'

'Seventeen.'

'Just a minute, seventeen-year-olds can't be sexually abused by a woman who looks like a film star!'

'But she had teeth sharper than razors. Every time she did it, I was worried sick she'd slice my nob off.'

Then Lenny began to grin. Then laugh. Then cough.

'You've started smoking again, haven't you?'

'No, but I miss it badly. I keep having this dream where a hand appears out of the dark and offers me a packet of twenty. I take one, but the cig keeps coming. Soon it's three feet long.'

Lenny mimed a cigarette between his fingers and then sat quietly, staring into space. At this point I noticed a very tinny black-coloured figurine of a horse and rider on the kitchen table.

'What's this?' I said, nudging the model with a finger.

'A bogie sculpture.'

'A what?'

'A bogie sculpture. It's made of snot.'

'You're having me on?'

'No, everyone picks their nose, but I pick mine for a reason. I model the snot and grade it: 1. Black and hard, 2. Stringy and gooey, 3. White and soft. The white and soft is the best.'

Lenny picked up the little figurine.

'There're two major disadvantages when modelling with snot,' he continued, authoritatively. 'Firstly, the things you can make with it are always tiny due to the smallness of the average snot crop. Secondly, there's never much detail, because snot has a tendency to crumble when dry. But I've made all sorts of figures from it – horses, cats, birds, you name it.'

And there they were all along the top of the bread bin. The horse was amazingly horse-like and the cat even had a grin on its face.

'What are you going to do with them all?'

'Well, this year I thought I'd send them out as Christmas presents. I was going to send you the cat. You can take it now if you like.'

'You think you're funny, don't you?'

15. Goodbye

Random Thoughts And Themes – priceless history II. Archduke Ferdinand of Austria was so vain that to avoid displaying any creases in his clothes he often had himself sewn into them. But when he was shot in Sarajevo in June, 1914, because his uniform could not be unbuttoned and because scissors could not be found in time, he bled to death.

On Monday I travelled across to The Heath again to say goodbye to Kim and Richard, but by the time I'd arrived they'd already left. So I raced back through the hospital – I just couldn't believe that Kim could leave without seeing me.

I found them in the car park. Kim had loaded Richard into the back of a new-looking estate car and was just settling herself down in the driver's seat.

'I was wondering where you'd got to,' said Kim.

'New car?' I said, trying to sound matter-of-fact.

'Yes, all part of the award.'

'Looks expensive.'

'It wasn't cheap, but we need some decent transport.'

'So you've said your goodbyes then?'

'Oh, Dean, you should have seen them – they lined everyone up and waved to me, I cried.'

'I can do a good *Gracie Fields*, you know.'

'What – the frock, the hair, the whole thing?'

'Oh, the hair's amazing – all those ringlets …'

'Hey, guess what – I've got a job!'

'Kim, that's great!'

'And it's paid!' It's at a citizens' advice bureau. Only two days a week, but that's all I want at the moment.'

'Excellent.'

I had nothing more to say now and wanted her to go. I was slightly naffed-off that she'd almost left without saying goodbye to me.

'Now you're definitely coming down to see us, aren't you, Dean?'

'Of course.'

I lied. But Kim knew this, because she was lying too. She wasn't asking me to visit her, she was saying goodbye.

When she'd gone I went back to the ward. I tried to read to Eva for a while but it was useless, I just couldn't concentrate, so I went down to the hospital canteen.

I didn't do much cooking at home, so it was nice once in a while to have a binge. And there was no better place to binge cheaply, than the The Heath canteen. For as canteens go, it was first-rate. There you could have truffled chicken breast with macadamia nuts, or beef teriyaki with bonfire beans, followed by a slice of angel cake and chased down with a cup of mint tea. And as the canteen was heavily subsidised, that lot would cost you £1.50 each for the main dishes and 30p for the side dishes and dessert. As a result the canteen was so popular that most of the time, it was difficult to get a seat. That day I had Camembert Frit, which was fried cheese with apple and Calvados jelly; La Salade de l'Hôpital – a great mound of warm pasta, roasted peppers, herbs and olives, and a wedge of Gâteau au Chocolat.

'Hungry, or eating disorder?' said Manika, a staff nurse.

'Hungry and greedy,' I said, sitting down beside her.

'Your council meeting was on the radio this morning. Tell me, is the Alton Estate such a great place to live in?'

'Not especially, but it's a community now and that's what matters.'

'Have you talked to them, Dean? Have you actually talked to the council?'

'Over the years we've talked the whole thing inside out. The problem is they've made up their minds and now they won't consider any other script.'

At this point, by mistake, instead of scooping up a forkful of pasta, I scooped up a Camembert-smeared forkful of Gâteau au Chocolat. Manika grinned.

'Just a sec,' I said, 'this tastes good …'

16. Labyrinth

Random Thoughts And Themes – things that I hate. Dogs that wag their tails at any human irrespective of whether they know them or not. Cuban heels. January and February.

That afternoon, I returned home to a battle. In the kitchen, Rachel and Nose were fighting over a cockroach. Each had a piece of the insect in its mouth and were circling one another, with Ken refereeing from the top of the fridge.

The problem was that up until the arrival of the hedgehog, the flat's unofficial insect population had been the gecko's exclusive playmates/eats. That she should now have to share them with another was something she seemed unable to consider. Though at that moment the problem was temporarily solved as the cockroach snapped in half. Crisis over, I slipped up to the sixth floor.

Vile's front door, for some reason, stood wide open. I called out, but there was no reply. Then all at once, Claire came bounding out of the distance and Vile appeared at the top of the hallway, with a glass in hand.

'The door was open,' I said.

'Really?' said Vile.

His voice was slurring so much I was afraid his tongue was going to slip and hurt itself. Up until then I don't think I'd ever seen Vile drunk. Out of his mind with skag, yes, but not Brahms and Liszt. In the kitchen, he leaned back in his chair, drained his glass and banged it down on the table.

'Have I ever shown you my plantation?'

Drunk or not, Vile knew full well he hadn't shown me

his plantation. No-one had had that privilege.

'Want to see it?'

'Might be interesting,' I said.

We took the lift down to basement level 1, which was as far as it would go, then got out and took the stairs. Here there was a strong smell of dust and piss.

At basement level 2, we came to a set of padlocked steel doors, where Vile took a bunch of keys from his pocket.

'Does Webley know about this?' I asked.

'I haven't the faintest idea.'

The steel doors were unlocked and pulled open, sending a booming sound echoing up the staircase behind us. Vile then tugged at a cord, a fluorescent blinked on and there stood an old wrought-iron spiral staircase. Here the piss stench was particularly serious.

'Place stinks …' I said.

'It's the sewers,' said Vile, 'they're all smashed to hell.'

Basement level 3 was full of abandoned bits of plumbing of every kind – boilers, fans, radiators, ducting. And neatly dividing the floor into two – an open sewer, running as swiftly as a small river.

'That's because it is a river,' said Vile. 'The Roe – joins the Thames at Kingston.'

Then I recognised my salt water plant outlet, which poured into the river from a hole in the ceiling. This was something Hillary had fixed up for me. I wondered why she hadn't mentioned the Roe, but then, perhaps like me, she'd thought it was a sewer.

Basement level 4 had a network of rooms full of splintery desks and filing cabinets.

'When I first came down here there was a ton of this old MOD stuff,' said Vile, kicking at a desk, 'but the dossers have taken most of it.'

'Where do the dossers live exactly and do they ever give you any trouble?'

'Most of them live at the back of level 2, and no, they've

never bothered me.'

In the last room, we came to a corridor and then I noticed that it was becoming noticeably warmer and that the dust and piss stench had been replaced by a strong, sweet smell.

At the end of the corridor, Vile opened another steel door and I gasped, for ten feet below me stretched a space the size of an aircraft hangar, where tungsten halogen lamps blazed and hissed above thousands and thousands of slender white and purple opium poppies. It was like looking down onto an Afghanistan mountain side. This was artificial plant breeding on an incredible scale.

'Vile, it's unbelievable ...'

He smiled. 'It's taken me nearly three years to get it like this.'

'How many individual plants are there, exactly?'

'Just under six thousand.'

When we got down to the floor level it was even more impressive, for many of the opium plants were over five feet tall and here the sweet smell was overpowering.

'Caring for them must be an enormous amount of work?'

'It was at the beginning, taking up the floor and creating a topsoil. But I did it bit by bit and now the only serious work I do is replacing dead plants and collecting the resins.'

'The resin collecting must be a big job.'

'Not really. Look closely and you'll see that the plantation is divided into three. So I only ever harvest a third of what you see here.'

And as I stared out at the field, I could see that this was true. The white and purple poppies, which looked like huge, floppy-winged butterflies, were blossoming fully only on one third of the plantation. The second section had flowers that were almost open. The third, just emerald-coloured buds.

We walked across to the middle of the plantation, where a set of tap heads were set into the floor. Vile crouched down and began turning the taps on. There was a knocking sound as water began to race through pipes all around us and then all at once, lukewarm water monsooned from the ceiling. In seconds we were soaked.

'I really needed this!' I shouted.

'Just as well then!' Vile shouted back, grinning.

After about a minute, Vile turned the rain off.

'And the advantage of opium plants,' he said, 'is that they are very hardy. All they really need is water, an even temperature, a bit of light, and they'll grow virtually anywhere.'

'What's the weight of the yearly opium harvest?'I said, wringing out my shirtsleeves.

'Not as much as you might think. Because some of the plants don't crop well, as when all said and done, these are artificial conditions. But have a look at this.'

Vile led me to the back of the plantation to an old urinal. 'What about that?' he said, pointing.

I put my head in the doorway and goggled. For standing in the corner, beside a row of urinal bowls, was the largest Venus flytrap plant I'd ever seen. It had leaves nearly a foot across and stood almost 6ft tall. It was a triffid. 'It's not possible,' I said. 'They never ever grow more then about 18 inches tall.'

'It's my ratter,' said Vile.

'How did you grow this?' I demanded.

'Do you remember giving me a flytrap about five years ago?'

'Vaguely. Actually, I don't even keep them any more. They kept dying on me.'

'Well, I just kept taking cuttings from stems that had the largest leaves and shoving them under tungsten. I've experimented with a few composts as well.' 'This cannot be a sexually mature plant?'

'Yes, it's spado, but remind me to show you a few slides I've made up. You'll find them interesting.'

'This place is sci-fi – The Lost World Of Witley ...'

Returning through level 2 a strange thing happened – we

bumped into a woman. She was about thirty years old, very thin and dressed in clothes that were almost rags. When she saw us, she scampered behind a large pile of rusty piling, like a big, scruffy mouse.

'One of the dossers,' said Vile.

I followed Vile as he led me behind the steel piling, where the basement widened out and all at once there were old armchairs, sofas, mattresses and a strong smell of cooking fat and shit. In one corner I could make out two elderly men sleeping, in another a man, perhaps Vile's age, sitting at a rickety table. His hair was matted and his nails glossed with filth. He glared at us.

'Up your arse,' he said, staring. 'Up your arse …'

17. One Until Two

Random Thoughts And Themes – memorable buildings. A Wendy house at primary school which I never went inside because for some reason I was too shit scared. A public toilet in Putney where once a man stood beside me and kept looking down at my knob and smiling. The Camden Parkway Cinema, because it's such a beautiful art deco building turned into a naff postmodern one.

That day I had a meal with Hillary.

'I hope you're hungry,' she said.

'I could eat a restaurant,' I said.

Frankly, after the meal at the hospital and the stench and filth of Witley's dossers, the last thing I felt like doing was eating. But good friends are precious and besides something hot and oily was spitting aggressively under the grill which had an interesting aroma. I sat down at the kitchen table and stared at the screen of Hillary's old Amstrad 8256.

'Is this the book?'

Hillary nodded. She was writing a book about out of body experiences. She was deeply into all that stuff. I read the paragraph on the green screen:

On the physical plane, out of body experiences, especially flying, can relate to erection and coitus. However, the astral body is an experience which is often closely related to death and may well be a survival response mechanism. Many people believe that if there is a survival from death then the out of body experience precipitates it. These experiences also strengthen the resolve that there is a possibility that one can survive death itself. This explains the emphasis on regarding the astral body as a light and dark experience.

'Oh, by the way, I hope you like fish?' said Hillary.

'I'll eat anything, as long as it's stopped moving,' I said.

Hillary smiled and laid two dinner plates side by side on the oven's hob.

'I had a bad experience today.'

'Oh yes?' I said.

'I found our cat dead in the garden.'

'Missile, dead?'

Hillary nodded.

'What did he die of?'

'Old age, I think. I don't know how Francine's going to take it, though.'

'She'll be all right. These things happen. How is she, by the way?'

'She's great. She's doing a drawing project at the moment. She has to sketch anything that is Victorian.'

'I feel as if I haven't seen her in months.'

'She was asking about you this morning.'

'Really?'

At this point, Hillary slid out the grill tray. Across it lay four fish. Carefully, she transferred these onto the dinner plates and plonked one down in front of me. I stared down at it.

'Flying fish?' I said.

'Yes,' beamed Hillary. 'Ever had them before?'

I didn't answer. I couldn't answer. I just gazed down at two silver bodies brushed with blue and yellow. My meal looked like a Chagall painting.

'Pretty, aren't they?' said Hillary.

I nodded, then lifted a fork and pulled a wing open. This was almost transparent. Where it wasn't transparent, it was pearly white. I let go and the wing flicked closed like a lady's fan. Oh, and another thing – they had huge eyes, these flying fish, huge, sad, blue eyes.

After our Abstract Expressionist lunch, I checked Hillary's electrical sockets. This was the main reason for my visit, as I was the block's unofficial electrician.

'Did you say you wanted another socket over here?' I said.

I was in the sitting room, underneath the balcony window.

'Yes, please,' said Hillary, 'by the TV.'

'Single gang, or double?'

'Could I have a double?'

I made a note of this on a scrap of paper. I was anxious to do this for Hillary as she'd helped me with a good deal of plumbing, particularly in the Fish Room, and I felt I needed to pay her back a bit.

After we'd completed the list, we sat down and had a cup of coffee. Then Hillary asked if she could do a reading for me. Now I wasn't sure, because the last time she'd read my cards, she'd ended up crying.

'Only if you don't get too emotional,' I said.

Hillary laughed. 'I won't. But The Tarot is a very emotional
 thing, you know.'

Who really wants to know the future? That's what I want to know. The past and present are heavy enough for most as it is – who wants to be told it's not going to change, or perhaps get even nastier? But there I was clearing the kitchen table.

'Firstly, I want you to pick out twenty-one cards,' said Hillary, shuffling the tarot pack and handing it to me.

I took seven cards from the top of the deck, seven from the bottom, and seven from the middle. Hillary sorted these into seven batches of three, then turned the first batch over – the Three of Cups, the Eight of Swords and a beautiful looking card called The World.

Unlike many tarot packs which have designs that are morbid, Hillary's had friendly faces looking out from every card. For instance, The World was painted in the shape of the planet bristling with life – in Australia a friendly duck-billed platypus waved at India, where a smiling tiger waved back.

'This choice shows that you are looking for approval,'

said Hillary, 'and that your main interests are intellectual. But someone is making strong emotional demands on you.'

'A woman?'

'Could be …'

My second choice was the Knight of Cups, the Four of Swords and the Devil. The Devil card showed a rakish-looking figure, sporting a handlebar moustache and a toothy grin, rather like Terry Thomas, the old British film actor.

'You are investigative …' said Hillary, 'you travel all sorts of routes through academia and you're irritated by the illogical, but have a deep longing for peace and contentment.'

Hillary was purring. She loved this sort of things, though it was beyond me as I tended to find all card games terribly boring. The Queen of Swords and the Queen of Rods appeared.

'Again I see a woman. She wants to give you love, Dean.'

'Who is she, for Godsake? Tell her I'm available, will you, please?'

'Again there's lots of emotion here.'

'By the way, I haven't told you, have I? Kim's moved to Plymouth and has invited me down to stay. I wonder if she's the woman?'

'Possibly.'

'Oh, it's all so hopeless, though. Plymouth is too far away and I'm scared stiff …'

'Of what?'

'I think she feels sorry for me. Even though she's cared for Richard for years, I've this feeling that she's just being kind and isn't serious.'

'Have you asked her out?'

'No.'

'How are things between you?'

'Good. Very good.'

'Why don't you just go along and see what happens?'

Hillary turned over the first card of the last pile. It was the Death card, but it didn't have the traditional skeleton design that everyone remembers. Instead it showed a child holding a moth, standing beside a grave.

'This is not a bad card,' said Hillary. 'The Death card is a card of change.'

Suddenly I felt warm. Very warm. And somewhere deep down inside me a bell began to ring. This was a small, shiny thing, with a clear bright sound. Then Hillary turned over the last but one card. This was the Tower and showed a castle being split in half with an enormous axe. Hillary frowned.

'Now this is what I would call a bad sign,' she said. 'It's the card of demise, sickness and shattered illusions.'

'Tell me something nice, please,' I pleaded.

'Don't worry. This hand is okay ... It's fine,' she said in an unconvincing tone of voice.

I closed my eyes as the last card was turned. When I opened them Hillary was smiling widely. The card was the Star.

'This is the card I'm most pleased to see here,' she said.

And with that, her eyes began to fill. Here we go, I thought.

'The Star is the card of hope and trust, Dean. It's really positive.'

'Thank God for that.'

And all at once, Hillary threw her arms around me and began to cry.

'You're going to win, Dean! You're going to win!'

'Look, I'm not trying to change the subject or anything,' I said, which was a lie, 'but I keep forgetting to tell you that I've seen The Cape.'

Hillary released me at once. She had a fascination with The Cape and liked to keep tabs on him.

'Where and when?' she said, looking grave.

'The beginning of last week. He was abseiling down the side of the building, holding onto himself.'

'Holding onto himself?'

'Yes, holding onto himself.'

Hillary had seen The Cape more times than anyone. In

fact, once she'd caught him wanking all over her kitchen window, while dangling from the outside of the building.

'You know, it's really worrying,' she said, 'there he is swinging about, flashing and tossing off today, but what will he get up to tomorrow? That's what I want to know. Did you call the police?'

'What can they do, Hillary? They'll just tick him off and let him go. If they manage to catch him, that is.'

'I'm terrified that one day he'll kill himself, sliding down the side of the building like he does.'

Just then the front door opened and suddenly there was Francine, standing in the kitchen doorway.

'Oh, look at the time, I didn't realise it was so late,' said Hillary.

'Hello, Dean,' said Francine, smiling.

She clasped me around the neck and we kissed each other on the cheek.

'Are you well?' I said.

She nodded.

'Put your case down and come here please, darling,' said Hillary.

Francine did as she was told and Hillary took her daughter into her arms.

'Now I've got something to tell you. And it's not good news, I'm afraid. Missile has died. Your little Missy is dead.'

'Missy's dead?' said Francine, without a trace of emotion.

'Yes.'

'Why did he die?'

'Because he was very old.'

'Where is he now?'

'I buried him in the daffodil garden by the playground.'

Francine looked out of the window, as if to see the playground with the daffodil garden and the grave.

'His body will start to rot now,' she said confidently.

'That's not very nice.'

'The maggots will eat his eyes first.'

'FRANCINE …!'

'It's true. A gerbil died at school, so Miss Tate put him in a jar with some maggots and they ate his eyes first.'

'That's awful.'

'Is there any Jungle Juice?'

Francine pulled away from her mother and opened the fridge door.

'Eyes first,' I said, 'could be worse.'

Hillary pulled a face at me, as Francine took a carton of Jungle Juice over to the draining board and selected a glass.

'He did live to a fair old age, though …' said Hillary, 'but then I suppose fifteen isn't that old for a cat. Your grandma had a cat that lived to seventeen, didn't she, Francine?'

But Francine was too engrossed in pouring herself a drink. When she had done this, she immediately drank the glassful of juice straight down, not even pausing to breathe.

'Do you have to drink like that?' said Hillary.

'Mummy, what's for tea?' said Francine, breathlessly.

'Marinated artichokes. And put that glass in the sink, please.'

'Afters?'

'Star Fruit à la Mélange …'

When I finally got back upstairs, it was early evening and Ken, my tabby, wanted to talk to me about something. But before I could oblige the phone rang. It was Ishmael. Bim had been found badly beaten up behind the rehab centre.

18. I Before the Storm

Random Thoughts And Themes – a great film that has never been made. The story of Baz, the man over the sweet shop on the Alton Estate, Roehampton, because he was on hazardous duties during the Second World War and once shot up an E-boat in his Motor Gun Boat.

Next morning as I sped along Roehampton Road, I was suddenly engulfed in a storm of dead leaves. Autumn – if it were not for all that death and ruin, it would be my favourite season.

Four-wheel-drive and Ishmael met me at the main gate of Queen Mary's Hospital. Queen Mary's stood about half a mile from Roehampton and was a vast, dusty, Edwardian honeycomb.

Bim's attackers had done a good job. They'd blacked his eyes and broken his nose and three fingers. Unbelievably, they had even, like some calling card, scratched the initials AB across his forehead. We three sat around the bed and watched as Bim slipped in and out of consciousness.

'This cannot be left …' said Four-wheel-drive, his voice booming in the box of the room.

'Right …' said Ishmael, nodding.

'Meaning?' I said.

But before Four-wheel-drive could answer, a police constable pushed through the doorway.

'Morning,' he said.

But Ishmael and Four-wheel-drive were already leaving, spinning their chairs around and pushing hard towards the doors, almost knocking the PC over.

'Your friends aren't too friendly,' said the copper, as the doors swung shut.

'They're angry,' I said.

'About Bim?'

The policeman leaned forward. He was perhaps a year older than I was.

'Do you know who did this?' he said, conspiratorially.

By 10am, I was on my way back to the village. In the High Street, I parked the chair outside the dry cleaner's, got out my sticks and slowly climbed the stairs to the dental surgery above.

In the reception, a girl was sorting through a pile of magazines.

'Mr McAdam?'

I nodded, she scored my name from a big black diary and I sat down next to a large fish tank. Inside the tank a single angel fish circled an ornament – a tacky, silver-coloured, plastic galleon.

'It's because he's so aggressive,' said the girl.

'Sorry?' I said.

'You were wondering why he's in there all on his own. It's because he's so aggressive. He fights every other fish we put in with him.'

I turned and stared at this solitary bruiser. He looked like an ordinary, peace-loving angel to me. A buzzer sounded.

'Dean ...' said Kalid Sachdev, extending a muscular arm and grinding my fingers gently together. 'Welcome ...'

I smiled, though it was a small one. I know it's childish and even clichéd, but I hate going to the dentist more than anything. Even the smell of the place makes me want to throw up. Kalid Sachdev had been my dentist for about four years and in that time we'd become quite friendly. But have you ever noticed how you never get *that* friendly with your dentist? I think it's a certain suspicion that holds us all back.

Deep down we realise that anyone who spends all day with his or her hands in the mouths of strangers administering pain and discomfort and claiming that they enjoy their work, has got to be suspect. I sank into the dentist's chair, the arms of which seemed to open and close around me.

'Are you well?' said Kalid, as he scanned my notes.

'Not too bad.'

'Any problems?'

'Not with my teeth ...'

'Any other problems?'

'Oh, you know how it is ...'

'The council pulling down The Alton?'

'Well, that's partly it.'

'It's a bad idea ...'

'There are a lot of them about these days.'

Kalid snapped a paper mask around his face.

'Well, I've got some good news,' he said, in muffled tones, 'I'm getting married on Saturday.'

'Honestly?'

'That's why I'm on my own. Razia is preparing our wedding.'

'Excellent!'

I tried to picture Razia and got a blurry image of a small Asian woman with large, smiling eyes.

'Yes, this is a very happy time for me, Dean. In two days I will be on my honeymoon.'

'Congratulations!'

Kalid tied a plastic bib around my neck and then picked up an angle mirror.

'And open ... So how is your hygiene regimen?'

'YYHHHAA ...'

'Are you keeping up with the flossing and the sticks?'

'YYHHHAA ...'

'Good, your gums look much better. Only one more filling to do, I see.'

Kalid put the angle mirror down and took up a large hypodermic from a kidney dish. I shifted in my seat. The dentist released the air from the syringe and a jet of pink-coloured fluid fountained from its tip. I gripped the arms of the chair again.

'Now just a little pinprick …'

The needle sank deep into my lower jaw. I closed my eyes and tried to think of nothing. But it's hard to think of nothing when someone is doing something awful to you. Seconds later the needle withdrew. It only hurts, I told myself, when the needle is withdrawing.

'Now we'll give that a minute.' said Kalid. 'Yes, how things change when you are in love. But I tell you, love is so powerful, it's like death …'

I nodded to this as Kalid picked up the probe again and passed the time while waiting for the anaesthetic to kick in by picking at a crusting of tartar at the back of my throat. It was a while before I realised that he was humming a tune, which sounded suspiciously like *Bednobs and Broomsticks*, though I couldn't be absolutely sure. Eventually I was told to rinse my mouth out.

'Is your mouth numb now?'

I touched my cheek. It felt like touching someone else's cheek. Shyly, I withdrew my embarrassed finger.

'YYHHHAAA …'

'Good … And open …'

The robot tendon elongated as the dentist lifted the drill from its hook. He swung the whole device into the back of my mouth, pressed the foot control and the drill screamed.

At about 2pm I scooted up to the sixth floor to see if Vile could spare me some food. I'd run out of money and my giro was still two days away.

'Sure you won't have some toast?'

'No, I'm fine,' I said.

We were sitting in the kitchen, sipping coffee, while Claire nuzzled Vile with her great wet nose. Vile began to stroke the dog's back hard, the giant toza whimpered ecstatically.

'What are you doing on the Battle Floors these days?' I said.

Vile looked up. His black mood of the previous day had completely vanished.

'Funny you should mention that, because I've just completely revamped the eighth. Fancy a game?'

'Of what?'

'Stag Planes.'

'Stag Planes?'

'It's new …'

19. Battle Floor!

Random Thoughts And Themes – memorable footwear. My sister's purple and silver platform shoes. My mother's yellow Wellington boots. My first pair of baseball boots, which hurt because they didn't really fit me. Consequently, I spent two months in such pain that I was cursing and swearing all the time, just like Joe Pesci in Good-fellas.

Only the first six floors of Witley Tower were occupied. So Vile used some of the abandoned floors as 'play environments'. And the games he played there could be fun. Models were his penchant – planes, boats, cars, etc, until he revealed this scheme, which for scale alone was impressive.

He'd completely cleared the eighth floor of all its dwellings and partitioning, leaving a rectangular space of 100ft square. This was then divided into two areas – the Blue Country and the Red Country. Using clay and plaster of Paris, Vile had constructed two miniature nations. Each model country had a capital city, towns, a port, an oil refinery and were separated by a thick band of blue sea. It was all schematic, but as a piece of scale-modelling, skilfully done and easily Vile's best effort so far.

'So where's the combat element?'

'Over here,' said Vile.

He led me to a table where two small model planes lay, one blue and one red. These had wingspans of about 18 inches and were propelled by tiny ½cc petrol engines. But as I looked at them closely, a movement caught my eye. Inside the perspex cockpit of each model, like tiny pilots, sat a live stag beetle. This was Vile's little joke.

'Radio-controlled with at least six channels, I presume?' I said.

'Eight channels,' corrected Vile.

He then explained that each plane carried fuel for a flight of twelve minutes and three tiny bombs hooked under the fuselage. Very carefully, he uncoupled one of these. It was made out of an old Vicks nasal spray capsule and contained a very small amount of pure nitroglycerine.

'At a touch from channel seven, a bomb will be released, detonate on impact, and blow a hole through wood, two thirds of an inch thick,' said Vile.

'Just three bombs,' I said. 'That's not going to go very far.'

But in truth I was impressed and I was having difficulty hiding it.

'You'll notice,' said Vile, 'that each plane carries a streamer. If that is in any way destroyed or shortened during the battle, that loses you points. And each country possesses three Calor Gas ack-ack emplacements, which when lit will shoot out a jet of flame about 4ft long.'

'So the objective is to attack the enemy country with the stag plane,' I said, 'defend your own territory with the Calor ack-ack, and the player to inflict the most and suffer the least is the winner?'

'With a coda,' said Vile. 'Destroy your opponent's plane and no matter what your overall score, you win. Simple as that.'

'Two questions – what's the battle duration and do I get any practice time?'

'Combat duration – ten minutes, with two minutes' practice. What country do you fancy?'

'Red's your colour, Vile.'

After lighting the Calor ack-ack emplacements, Vile launched each plane by starting their motors and simply chucking them into the air. The $\frac{1}{2}$cc engines made an incredible racket. Predictably, the vibrations sent the stag beetle pilots crazy.

'Remember!' shouted Vile over the din. 'Channel 7 is the bomb release. They'll go front first!'

I stared down at my handset. It was amazing just how sensitive my model was. If I asked it to lower its flaps – in other words to dive – it did so instantly. Though I soon realised that it was better to have the plane flying in a wide circle all the time, then I could spend more time thinking about exactly what I was going to do.

'One minute to go!' crowed Vile.

I also soon realised that the Calor ack-ack were not very manoeuvrable. For one thing, the control to lower the barrel had a two-second delay on it. So I decided to have these pointing straight up, then all I had to worry about was extending the flame.

'Thirty seconds!' yelled Vile.

One interesting thing about the two miniature countries was that each city had blocks like the TV station, Post Office, Parliament building. Hits in these zones scored heavily. Vile had really thought this out.

'7,6,5,4,3,2,1 GOOOOOOOOOOOOOOOO!!'

This was brilliant. For just as the battle began, my plane swung around for a pass directly above Vile's Red City. So I took a chance and pressed channel 7. A nitro bomb leapt from my bomber's undercarriage, fell quickly and burst smack in the middle of the city. The bang was like a firework exploding. Smoke began to chimney from the TV station.

'SHIT!' cried Vile.

I burst out laughing. So much so, that for a second I lost concentration and my model coasted so near the windows of the building that I swear for a moment it scraped along glass. But I pushed hard on the flap control and the blue plane swooped across the room, just as Vile's model swept along my coastline and released a bomb. There was another bang and a small ball of fire lashed across my port. I swung my Calor ack-ack and blasted the flame out, but I was way off target.

'TAKE THHHHHHAT!!' screamed Vile. 'WATCH OUT,

BLUE BOY, THE REDDLE MAN IS ON YOUR TAIL!'

And he wasn't joking, for Vile's bomber climbed hard, looped across the room, came up behind my plane and ripped my streamer to shreds.

'HEY, I THOUGHT YOU HADN'T PRACTISED!' I howled.

'I NEVER SAID THAT!' laughed Vile.

Again I went in for an attack, diving my plane towards the Red City, pulling up at the last moment and letting a bomb go. But this time, the explosive burst harmlessly between two towns.

'RUBBISH!' sneered Vile.

Then his model came around the back of the Blue Country and released two bombs. It was an incredible shot. The deadly Vicks capsules ripped right across my city, setting it completely ablaze. Flukily, some of the flaming nitro even dripped down a road and set my port smoking. Suddenly I was in bad shape – half of my country was on fire or smouldering.

'WHAT A HIT!!' bawled Vile.

'PURE LUCK!!' I shrieked back.

Vile had used all of his bombs now, but I still had one left, and this last shot had to be good. I had already hit his city, so as his port and oil refinery were in a line, I attacked in that direction, sure to hit something. I was really getting the hang of handling the bomber now. I had it diving and banking all over the place. I just wished the practice time had been longer. Zipping along the Blue Country's coastline, my plane crossed the partitioning sea, reached the Red Port and my last nitro capsule hurtled downwards. There was a louder than usual bang and a shower of clay and plaster of Paris leapt into the air. The bomb had hit, not the Red Port, but the Red Oil Refinery.

'Must have been extra ni in that one!' hollered Vile.

Both countries were now heavily ablaze. Particularly mine. And there was a choking stench of petrol and gas everywhere. What with all the smoke and flame, it was getting difficult to see exactly what was going on. Then I made a bad mistake. As my plane climbed over the Red City, there was a sudden jet of flame from a Calor ack-ack and all at once my blue model was on fire, nose to tail.

'HAAAAAAAAAAAAAAA!!!' bellowed Vile, jumping up and down.

But then an amazing thing happened. Virtually out of control, my maimed bomber veered across the room and cracked the red plane square in the arse. If I'd planned it for a year, I couldn't have wished for better, for the red model immediately spun out of control, smashed through a window and plunged out of the block in a shower of glass and flame.

'You jammy tosser!' protested Vile.

'Game to me, I think,' I said.

'Nonsense, your country is a piece of charcoal.'

'But I destroyed your plane.'

'I'll give you a draw.'

We doused the smoking debris, opened some windows to let some fresh air in and generally tidied up a bit. Gradually, the smoke and stink cleared. Vile and I peered out of the smashed window, but his model was nowhere. On the other hand, my bomber had glided to a neat halt in the sea between the two warring countries, where the stag beetle sat in the charred cockpit but was now very, very, still.

Back in Vile's kitchen, I leaned my sticks against the wall and rested. Not that I was tired. It was just that my pressure sores – gifts from my months in a hospital bed – were playing up again. As I massaged the backs of my legs, Claire suddenly rushed from Vile's bedroom barking excitedly. Around her neck was a frayed rope, a steel eye and a chunk of brick and plaster – the brute had broken free from somewhere. That dog was a menace! Vile appeared carrying two glasses and a bottle of something.

'Please, be quiet, Claire,' he said.

But the massive dog proceeded to yowl at the top of its

bark. If it had been me I'd have chained her up outside and as we were on the sixth floor, I'm sure that would have had a calming effect. However, Vile simply kicked her in the stomach, which seemed to do the trick.

'My father died two days ago,' said Vile, sitting down.

'So that's what the Jim Beam was all about?'

'It was a stroke. Do you remember my dad?'

Did I remember his dad? Vile's family were all completely unforgettable, particularly Ross, his father. His mother, my Aunt Olivia, was easily the most fascinating relation I had. With her Mediterranean good looks of pale skin, black eyes and long, shiny black hair she represented the height of sexual mystery for me as a child. She was always smoking, I remember that. Although smoking seemed to suit her, for she would light a cigarette and for a moment the smoke would cling to her face like a veil. But the king memory-limpet relation was Ross. No question. No-one meeting Ross De Vile would ever forget him, for he was the epitome of the *utter bastard*, the subject of many family stories, one of the nastiest of which I'm going to tell you now.

It begins with Olivia buying Vile and his brother Brian, who were then about ten and eleven respectively, a pair of Dutch white rabbits. Now right from the start the two boys were mad for these two lettuce-nibblers who quickly took over their lives. The main project, as it were, was to set about building a huge hutch and a system of passageways for the animals to live and play in. Which the boys did with great enthusiasm – the damn structure eventually spanned the length and breadth of the old barn. It was all very intense stuff. So when after six months the animals caught a fatal dose of coccidiosis, which is a virulent rodent respiratory disease, it was hello serious trauma.

This all took place in the family home in Dorset, which I visited several times as a boy. There Ross's study was a shrine to English public school machismo. The tosser had trophies everywhere – rowing, boxing, fencing, little boys' arses – it was all very gross, the English upper-middle class, they've a lot to answer for. So anyway, the vet was called to the rabbits, but nothing could be done as the coccidiosis was too advanced. So Ross announced that the animals would have to be put down, while strangely allowing the vet to leave without performing the job. That evening he took the two boys across to the old barn and thrust one of the sick rabbits into Vile's arms demanding he strangle it. He refused, but Psycho Dad insisted – as the eldest brother it was Vile's duty to put the rabbits out of their misery, he was told. The more delay, the more the creatures would suffer, etc, etc. Faced with that kind of emotional arm twisting, Vile killed the rabbit, as no doubt anyone would have done. Predictably, he was devastated by this insane cruelty, but that was typical of the sort of shite he had to put up with as a child, which probably had something to do with the dangerous stuff he got into as an adult, more of which you'll hear about later.

20. Animal Jinks

Random Thoughts And Themes – things that are sad. Sandwiches that just have cheese in them. The Isle of Wight. Petrol stations that only sell petrol. Appearing as a contestant on a TV gameshow.

This time when I returned to the flat, I found Nose and Rachel together again, but curled up in the wash basket. I cannot think of a more unlikely friendship then a hedgehog and a gecko. They are certainly at the opposite ends of the biogenetic scale. Ken was also having a snooze, stretched out across my bed. Actually, all the animals were sleeping, even the birds of prey, with one exception. My bat.

Since I had trapped her, she had not eaten properly and was by now quite weak. So I decided to put her back on the common – unfortunately, you can't force-feed small animals. And as I hadn't yet checked the traps for the day, I popped her into a specimen jar and zoomed over there and then.

Once more it had rained fairly heavily overnight, so the common was miry and thick with wet smells – wet birch, wet blackberry, wet puffball fungus. But as I approached the stream, I saw something odd whirling in an eddy. It was one of my traps. Then another floated by. I found more further on, scattered across the pathway. Next I found the first dead animal. It was a baby hedgehog, about the size of Nose. It had its belly slit open. There were also dead field mice on the bank, one of which was squashed flat inside a trap. Finally, someone had set fire to my two insect collectors. The destruction was total.

That evening, I had to open the centre up, which was unusual, because Ishmael and Four-wheel-drive were nearly always there before me. As I flicked the lights on, Lucy wheeled up the pathway.

'I've just come back from the hospital,' she said.

'How's Bim?'

'He's conscious now, and doesn't look too bad, although those black eyes don't help. Where are Four-wheel-drive and Ishmael?'

'I don't know.'

Lucy and I chatted, we didn't have the heart to do anything else, and by ten o'clock, still alone, we locked the building up and I saw her home. That took about twenty minutes, then I went looking for Four-wheel-drive and Ishmael, which took about three minutes.

'We missed you at the club,' I said.

'Been busy,' said Ishmael.

'Doing what?'

They were sitting in the dark on Blackford's Path. Of course, the situation had become too bad. To do nothing now would have been to show weakness and I don't know whether you've noticed, but showing weakness often excites callousness and cruelty.

'I'm just going down the snicket,' said Four-wheel.

I'd never seen Four look as he did then – eyes that were slits, bordered by dark rings big as saucers. Ishmael nodded as Four-wheel swung his chair around and pushed himself up the pathway and halfway along it, disappeared down a snicket.

Blackford's Path was an old village alleyway that linked the High Street with Medfield Street. It was tarred, perhaps fifty yards long, and at night, poorly lit. Most evenings the ABs Roehampton team would drink until late in The Angel on the High Street, then at closing time buy some chips from the chip shop opposite and walk through Blackford's to the Medfield Street end. There they would stand, eating their supper, and abusing anyone that passed by.

As we waited, I looked up at the dark, silent shape of

Addison's the ironmonger's at the top of the pathway. I could just make out the flaky old Philips' sign – *Ancient lights, Modern lights.*

It took an hour. Though the time passed quickly. It's odd how that happens in times of stress. One moment you're here, the next you're there, sixty moments later.

There were about six of them and they were in good spirits - laughing and shouting as they waltzed down the pathway. I recognised a small rat-faced boy called Degs, who was the nucleus of everything the ABs did in Roehampton, plus Two Para, a thickset Geordie, who always wore a grubby-looking flak jacket.

'So what did I do?' Degs yelled. 'I took out my dick and waved it at him ...'

The others screamed with laughter.

They were now almost halfway down the path, but still had not seen Ishmael and me. The odds were about 2 to 1. Which was unlucky. Unlucky for them. It would have been better if they'd had double their number. As they passed the halfway mark, Ishmael pushed himself into the centre of the alley and the meagre light from the single lamp-post caught the chrome frame of his chair and glinted. But the ABs were so engrossed with each other, they still didn't notice us. Then, only a few feet away, they stopped dead, not believing their luck.

'Fuck me up the arse with a candle, look who it is,' said Degs, 'a couple of musical chairs ...'

One or two of the gang sniggered. But they could see that Ishmael, with his broad powerful-looking chest and arms, was a completely different punter from Bim. But then there were six of them and two of us, weren't there? And, of course, we were in wheelchairs.

'You're cunts,' said Ishmael, 'scabby cunts that need binning ...'

The AB's grins vanished then and a tall boy with a scar under his left eye stepped forward. But in a movement that was a blur, Ishmael hurled his hands behind him, snatched the baseball bat that lay there and smashed it across the boy's head so hard that for a moment, I thought he'd killed him. The rest of the ABs leapt back. But they were moving far too slowly, for within another split-second, Ishmael had arched from his chair and felled another boy. The remainder turned to flee, only to find Four-wheel-drive blocking their way, holding an 18 inch breadknife up to the moon. He had slashed the faces of two before they knew what was happening. The bloody duo, like some grotesque double act, fell screaming. Degs and Two Para turned and literally leapt over the top of Ishmael and ran. While Four-wheel-drive dragged the one remaining boy to the floor, tore open his shirt and swiftly opened his chest up to the darkness.

That night as I was trying to sleep I heard a sound I didn't recognise. A low, distant drumming. As I listened to it, the building seemed to murmur softly in response and I shivered. Then I closed my eyes and immediately I was surrounded by LCDs and a glowing landscape of a red sky and gold precipice. I unfolded my massive arms – appendages, tons heavy – and START flashed in the corner of my eye. I began to walk.

I walked until I arrived somewhere. Eventually, I arrived in the countryside. There the ground slid open and I slipped into cool sheets of clay, pulling a soft blanket of grass around myself. Then Eva was floating above me, her torso made of glass. I could clearly see her red apple of a heart somersaulting over and over. I wept then. I turned my face to my pillow of clay and wept.

Then I was walking again.

I arrived somewhere once more. A deserted high street this time. Smashed lamp-posts sprawled and nuggets of glass glittered. I strolled past a row of shops and into a supermarket. An Asda, actually. Without thinking, I grabbed a trolley and began to breeze down the exotic aisles, tacking hard. I took everything – Wispa, Weetabix, Basmati, Malties, Delicat, Klear, Plax, Hax, Trix, Trax … I slumped against a counter, breathless and sweating. Then I ran from the ghost Asda into a nearby house. There I raced from room to room opening cupboards, desks, drawers, my wrists. Again I heard the drumming. No, it wasn't drumming, I realised, it was a padding sound. An animal was running towards me and it was big, very fucking big. Then the house folded into a long dark corridor and I began to run. I ran so fast it hurt – my lungs pulling like pumps. But the animal gained on me. So I ran faster. I ran beyond myself – a dream of speed. Yet still the animal gained. Then it was right behind me, the stench and heat of its breath on my back. I turned and a huge glinting mouth poured in a slipstream of drool. Suddenly I was cascading – a wall of liquids – blood, semen, saliva, piss, pus, tears.

21. After Maths

Random Thoughts And Themes – priceless football. Getting a real leather football for Christmas when I was about eight years old that was never inflated during its entire lifetime. Swapping a pair of football boots for two brass coins from India that had holes through their centres. Seeing a photo of Bobby Moore and not knowing who he was.

It was my signing-on day. I dressed quickly, fed the animals, went downstairs, and promptly bumped into Webley. I had a lot on that day, so this was a pain.

'That …' he murmured, nodding at my wheelchair.

'Yes?'

'Next time …'

'You'll …'

'Dump it … You've been …'

'Warned?'

'Warned.'

I smiled at him. And why shouldn't I? For I knew, as he obviously didn't, that when chained up on the ground floor, my wheelchair was wired to a 440 volt supply. So should he or anyone attempt to move it, or even touch it, they'd receive a charge likely to throw them so high in the air, they'd need a parachute or canonisation to get safely back down.

As I think I've already mentioned, I was soon to start at university. This studentship had been delayed for nearly two years because of the accident. During that time, to keep from starving or becoming a rentboy, I'd signed on. At first, I'd claimed sickness benefit. Then I switched to income support, as Jobcentres won't organise interviews for you if you're on the sick. But I really liked the idea of having a job. Well, I'd never had one before and it had a certain romantic ring to it, to be able to say – 'I have a job.' Though things hadn't quite worked out. I had been given the occasional interview, which usually went well, until the true extent of my disabilities became known. Nonetheless, I kept trying.

At the Roehampton Jobcentre I took my place in the queue as usual and waited. To be fair, I quite liked this Jobcentre, because it was warm, had easy access, para toilets and an almost friendly atmosphere (for a Jobcentre, that is). Though I was glad I only spent an average of about half an hour a week in it, otherwise I might have felt differently. Anyway, after the obligatory ten-minute wait, I was told that I might have to have a Restart Interview. So I crossed the room and joined another queue. There I was given the fearful news that the DSS wanted to see me. This was a particular pisser as it meant a trip to East Putney, which was 3 miles away, and as it was impossible to take my chair on the bus, I'd have to crutch it, which would take the best part of two hours.

The East Putney DSS was housed in an old sixties building, exceptional only for its unsightliness. But the smell was the worst. In the corridors it was stale urine and spew. In the reception room, fresh urine and fresh spew. Another reason I hated the building was the mountain of stairs that had to be climbed to get into it. And that morning, to top it all, when I eventually reached the front doors, two men stopped me and demanded money. But I was in no mood for any nonsense, so I looked threatening (I have six of these postures) pushed past them and went inside.

In the reception I took a ticket from the dispenser – number 51 – and looked up at the display – number 6. I swore and sat down.

There were some fifty people waiting in the room, half of whom were smoking, therefore, a thick, blue-grey fug drifted in the air. Darting beneath this smoke roof were perhaps six or seven young children. They raced around the room yelling and shouting. But my eye was caught by a woman dressed in Wellington boots, perhaps in her mid-fifties, who was walking back and forth, talking to herself. Sometimes her words ran together, sometimes not. It was all about the royal family and went something like this –

'Princess Anne's going to sea and good luck to her ... She likes the sea and the sea likes her and why shouldn't it? 'Course, Charles, he don't like the sea, 'cos he's not got sea legs. Mind you, he's got lofty legs. But he's always been lofty. Like his dad. But more weighty. More chunky ...'

When listening to this became tedious, which was quite soon, I pulled out my latest, *Beautiful Stories for Ugly Children*. This was a brilliant Canadian comic book that I'd been collecting. The writing was excellent and the graphics like nothing I'd ever seen before. I read a story about a little girl so taken with the beauty of her puppy's eyes that she plucked them out and strung them on a piece of string.

I waited four and a half hours at the DSS, only to find out that all they wanted to see me about was my address. Apparently, the post office had been returning my mail marked – *unable to deliver*. Briefly, I explained the situation at Witley – that it was getting difficult to receive mail – which seemed to satisfy the counter assistant, who then tapped a note into her VDU and told me that the Jobcentre wanted to see me back in Roehampton.

'Sorry?' I said.

'Yes, apparently there's a job possibility.'

When I finally arrived back at the Jobcentre, it was closing time.

'Dean, I've got an interview for you,' said, the desk clerk.

Even if I do say so myself, I was quite popular at the Jobcentre. Yes, the feel-sorry-for-you factor was high, which normally would have enraged me, but I let it go, simply because they had the worst jobs in the world, although they seemed not to know it.

'What is it, exactly?' I asked.

'Carriage cleaner for Railtrack.'

'Well, do you think I could do the job with one hand?'

'Sorry?'

'Well, I use crutches to walk with, you see. And I also use them to stand up with, of course.'

I lifted my armpits chimpanzee-like and bumped them up and down a bit.

'Look, why don't you go along and see what they say?'

When I got back home I heard some terrible news – Putney had got their eviction orders. Which was predictable, but more worryingly, Hillary, Francine and Mrs Dear had decided to move out that very evening.

Even though I'd known it was a good possibility – my friends leaving Witley – the reality was a shock. They called in to say goodbye and were obviously embarrassed, though it was okay by me, and I told them so. Hillary had to look after Francine and Mrs Dear wasn't very well – she had tinnitus, which I wouldn't wish on anyone. So there was nothing more to say. They had to leave and that was the end of it.

'Will you come and see us in Southfields, Dean?' said Francine.

Her little white face shone up at me at that moment and suddenly my heart dam-busted with fondness for her.

'Yeah,' I said, 'of course …'

I saw them down to the driveway, like some doting parent, where at the kerbside, Hillary's dad sat waiting inside an old Ford van. This was jammed with cardboard boxes full of clothes, bedding and odd pieces of furniture.

'We're leaving quite a bit of stuff behind,' said Hillary, handing me her keys. 'There's just no room at Mum and Dad's. But if things calm down a bit we'll be back.'

'Meanwhile, I'll keep an eye on all of it,' I said.

We all looked at each other then and were silent. Then they got into the van and as they drove down the driveway, I waved and they waved and I knew and they knew that they would never return to Witley Tower.

22. The Loneliness of the Long Distance Tower Block

Random Thoughts And Themes — silliness. One of my earliest memories of silliness is when I was about three years old, for it was then that I saw a picture book showing blackbirds fleeing from the inside of a huge pie, with clear expressions of panic written all over their faces. Bake live birds in a pie — what a silly idea, I thought.

For dinner, to cheer myself up, I did some cooking. This was not like me. It wasn't that I didn't like cooking. I did. It was just that ordinarily, I never had the time.

I cooked a vegetable curry and once I'd started, I suddenly wished I cooked more often. It was so relaxing. Then the phone rang.

'Heard?' said Lenny.

'That Putney have got the eviction orders?'

'So what are we going to do about it?'

'I don't see that we can do much. They'll arrive and try and throw us out and we'll resist. That's about it.'

'We can't just sit here and let it happen.'

'What else can we do?'

'It seems stupid to do nothing.'

'Look, I'll have a word with Vile and see if we can't organise a barricade or two.'

I rang Vile straight away and he agreed that we should put together one or two surprises for the council. An hour later, we met on the ground floor.

Firstly, we hauled a few old boilers and wardrobes up from the basements and pushed them up against the front and rear doors. Then we had a look at the stairways and here

Vile came up with a stylish, but rather dangerous idea –

'Suppose we demolish the stairs all the way to the first-floor landing. Then if we keep the lift on the first floor, no-one will be able to gain access to the building without climbing gear, or a helicopter.'

'But how do we get in and out of the building?' I said.

'One of us will always have to be inside. So you go down in the lift, exit, and who ever is left in the building calls the lift back up and jams the door open. Then when you want to come back up, you phone, or shout up to a window, and Lenny or I will send the lift back down.'

'Sounds fairly plausible. But how do we demolish the stairways. They're solid concrete.'

'With 15lb hammers, of course.'

And after a fashion, that's what we did. Although demolished stairs wasn't quite what we finished with (concrete is incredibly hard, even for a 15lb hammer) yet we made enough mess to render the stairs hazardous to use, which was the general idea. And just to make it even more uncomfortable, we took all the windows and the bannisters out as well. We laboured hard – about three hours each stairway, but the result was not unsatisfying.

I got back to the flat at about 1.30am, completely exhausted and covered in concrete dust. However, others were wide awake and full of energy as Nose and Rachel were running around playing tag. What really fascinated me about those two was that they seemed to have swapped behavioural traits. Nose was acting like a gecko and Rachel like a hedgehog. And all of this without any Happy Room conditioning. I made a note to consider setting up a trial and went to bed.

23. Br, It's Cold

Random Thoughts And Themes – the time just before waking. I think about this time quite a lot. I imagine myself in the hour before I wake as floating in a pool face down. Though it's not like swimming because I'm floating in sleep, where every now and then images like fish fin up from the blackness to meet me, touch and then streak back down to the dark again.

Early on the Friday morning I bused into Putney and caught the tube into town.

The train was crowded but at Parsons Green Station, a boy got on and sat next to me who had hair shaped to a point, standing up a full three feet from his head. I was reminded of a unicorn.

'Brilliant hair,' I said.

'Ta,' he said, smiling.

'How do you get it to stand up like that?'

'I just lacquer and comb it.'

'And it stands up all by itself?'

'Yeah'

The Unicorn Boy got off at West Brompton, bending his knees at the doorway so his hair wouldn't snap off.

At Euston Station, I had trouble finding the interview room. But eventually, at the back of the building, I came across a Portakabin with about fifteen people queuing outside.

'Looking for a carriage cleaning job?'

It was Ishmael.

'Ish, what are you doing here?'

'Same as you – looking for a job.'

'I didn't know you were on the dole.'

'I wasn't until last week, but no-one wants a tattoo at the moment. They're saving their skins for Christmas.'

Grinning, I joined the queue behind him, just as a smartly dressed woman, flanked by two security guards, arrived.

'Go inside, find a seat, and sit down,' said the woman, unlocking the door to the Portakabin.

'She looks a bit pale,' said Ishmael.

'Do you think so?' I said.

'It's the oxygen starvation. They're all time frozen, you know.'

Inside, the Portakabin was arranged like a classroom. Ishmael and I found desks adjacent to one another and when we were all settled, the woman introduced herself.

'Good morning, I'm Mrs Trinder, Senior Personnel Officer, and this is Mr Paul and Mr Peters.'

The two security men nodded, mutely.

'Now you're here today to be interviewed for carriage cleaner's jobs, is that correct?'

We all nodded.

'Good, now let's get on. We've got a lot of ground to cover.'

We then proceeded to spend the next thirty minutes filling out application forms and reading a pamphlet that told us all about Railtrack conditions of employment. Then we saw an old British Rail labour recruitment film. Although this nearly didn't happen, as the security men had trouble unravelling the film screen, for having heaved so hard, the screen suddenly ripped from its container.

There was laughter. Ishmael was beside himself. Ishmael had a very idiosyncratic laugh – a sort of high-pitched guffawing, with a little hiccup on the end. It was unmissable. Mrs Trinder certainly didn't miss it.

'Do you have to make that noise?' she said, indignantly.

'No,' said Ishmael, 'there's a whole range you can choose from.'

There was more laughter.

'You are serious about applying for a job here, I trust?'

'Of course,' said Ishmael, holding onto a straight face with all his might.

'Good', said Mrs Trinder, frowning, obviously making a mental note about Ishmael.

The mutilated screen was finally attached to a blackboard with drawing pins and the film show began. This described pensions, travel benefits and disciplinary procedures and was remarkable in that it was a piece of archive material, peopled by odd-looking characters wearing kipper ties, flowery shirts and Afro hairstyles. When the film came to an end, the lights flicked on and Mrs Trinder asked us if we had any questions. Ishmael put his hand up.

'About the disciplinary procedures ... If you receive a first warning, does it go on your record?'

'Certainly,' said Mrs Trinder.

'Could it affect your promotion prospects?'

'It would depend on the position you've applied for.'

'Well, say I was a carriage cleaner and I applied for a job as a ticket collector ...'

'Look, I don't want to get bogged down in that area. You'll have to consult a union rep for that sort of information. Now provided there are no further questions, we'll have a break before we continue.'

Thankfully, there were no more questions, so we all began to file out of the classroom and into a canteen next door.

'I think she likes you,' I said.

'Actually,' said Ishmael, 'I think I've fallen madly in love with her.'

Half an hour later, we were back in the Portakabin, where we were given a psychometric test. This consisted of fifty questions, some of which were related to the film we'd seen, while others seemed to be related to nothing in particular –

Take two apples from three apples. What do you have?

And –

How many animals of the same type did Moses take into the ark?

But my favourite was –

You drove a bus from Manchester with 45 people on board. Along the route you picked up 3, dropped off 5 and stopped for a half an hour break at Coventry. What was the driver's name?

When we'd all finished, Mrs Trinder collected the papers and then interviewed us one by one.

While these interviews took place, I sat in my seat looking at my hands. And I must say that sitting in a Railtrack Portakabin looking at your hands is so boring, it's dangerous to your health. Finally, after over an hour, Mrs Trinder got around to me but was puzzled.

'If you're going to college in three weeks, why have the Jobcentre sent you?'

'I could work weekends?' I said, enthusiastically.

'But it's full-timers we're looking for.'

'I could work full-time in the holidays?' I said, smiling.

At lunch-time, Ishmael and I went looking for something to eat. We found a little kebab house behind the station and bought a doner each.

'Good value, eh?' said Ishmael.

I had to agree. For the money, the doners were excellent. I squeezed a lemon quarter over a huge salad.

'What I like about these are the pittas – just gently toasted. I hate it when the pitta has been toasted hard.'

'I find you've got to be careful with kebab houses,' said Ishmael, licking a dribble of chilli sauce from his chin.

I nodded. 'I hardly ever go to a kebab house that hasn't been recommended.'

'When I was at school, there was this superb one just down the road from me. Fresh pitta. Fresh salad. Fresh lemon. Beautiful …'

'The salad's got to be right, hasn't it?'

'Plenty of tomato,' insisted Ishmael.

'And lemon … It gives more mileage to everything.'

'Absolutely …'

After lunch, we were shown some first aid techniques. Mrs Trinder provided the voice-over, while the two security guards performed the actions. Here we learned that for some reason the old British Rail had enjoyed one of the highest fatality rates of any state-run railway in the world. One contributing factor was thought to be a lack of first aid awareness.

'I hope to Christ we're getting paid for today,' whispered Ishmael. 'Imagine sitting through all of this and getting nothing at the end of it.'

'There are fares and luncheon vouchers, apparently,' I whispered back, 'but you don't get them unless you last the day.'

Finally, Mrs Trinder and her two assistants gave us some training in coping with someone who'd suffered a heart attack. It included several demonstrations on a life-size rubber doll. At the end of these, Ishmael put his hand up.

'What if you feel a heart attack coming on? What if you are the victim?'

There were a few chuckles.

'No, I'm serious,' insisted Ishmael. 'It could happen.'

'Get to the nearest telephone and call an ambulance,' said Mrs Trinder.

'But what if you've already collapsed?'

'Well, there's not much you can do in that case, is there? Except to keep calm until help arrives.'

'But what if help doesn't arrive?'

'Then you'll probably die!'

At the end of the day, thirteen people out of the fifteen were offered jobs as carriage cleaners. Guess who were the odd two? Ishmael and I collected our expenses – £4 – and then began wandering homeward.

'What's the time?' said Ishmael.

'4.20pm.'

Without another word Ishmael hailed a black cab.

It had been a long time since I'd ridden in the back of a London black cab. In fact, so long that I couldn't remember when I'd last done so. 'A bit lavish,' I said, settling back in the seat, 'especially as we're both utterly skint. Where're we going, by the way?'

'The Courtauld, on The Strand,' said Ishmael.

The gallery was not very crowded, as it was nearly closing time and most people were leaving. We paid the entry fee, which left me completely penniless and Ishmael led the way.

In the lift we passed the Italian section, the Spanish section, the English section and then at the Dutch section, on the fourth floor, we got out.

There, a few minutes later, in a large, softly lit room, we stood before a triptych. This was perhaps 6ft long and painted with an immense amount of detail – the right side depicted Paradise, the middle, Earth, and the left, Hell. On the side that depicted Hell, evil-looking animals prowled beneath a sky that was darkened by an insect-like host. But it was the right-hand side that was really impressive. For in the middle of the picture, underneath a lion-shaped marble fountain, the world's first man and woman knelt before a king. The couple were naked, had their hands clasped as if in prayer and were smiling up at the king, who was wearing a pink and gold robe. This little group was surrounded by a stunning landscape of trees, flowers and gentle-looking creatures. I read the inscription on the nameplate – 'The Great Garden, Hieronymus van Aken, 1460–1516'.

'Philip of Spain loved his paintings so much that he hung them all around his bedchamber,' said Ishmael.

And it was an impressive painting, no doubt about it.

Consequently, we stood looking at it for almost half an hour before the gallery closed.

That evening I stayed in. I was very tired and I needed to hold on pause for a while. But before I went to bed, I looked in on the Fish Room In the sea horse's tank, the male was still drifting calmly in the middle of the aquarium. No change there, I thought. As usual I went over and said hello to Julie and while doing so noticed that one of the shore crabs in her tank, Aldgate, had two legs missing. I wondered whether Julie had snacked on him, or whether he'd lost out fighting with another crab. But just then, I heard a popping sound. I looked back into the sea horse's tank to see the male give a violent flick and like an exploding piece of gothic jewellery, spray tiny transparent young everywhere. It was happening! I couldn't believe it! The sea horse was finally giving birth! I pulled up a chair and sat down – I didn't want to miss a thing, though disappointingly, within two minutes it was all over. I couldn't quite understand this, as I knew that a sea-horse birth can take hours. Nonetheless, I wasn't complaining and had to act fast before Dad got hungry, so I got a hand net, quickly scooped up all the fry and tipped them into a nursery tank.

I estimated that I had about eighty baby sea horses. Their transparency gave them a sort of ghostly look, so that when they burst into a spasm of movement, zipping backwards, in that unique sea horse way, they looked like tiny sea horse ghosts as they disappeared and reappeared, merging and re-emerging with the weed and rock of the tank.

I watched the baby sea horses until I couldn't keep my eyes open, then I went upstairs, flopped on my bed and dreamed of shafts of light streaming through cracks in my skull. Not an unpleasant dream, though not one I remember with particular fondness either.

24. The Phoney War

Random Thoughts And Themes – impressive insects II. Having your head severed in the insect world is not an uncommon occurence, consequently, it's been observed, on numerous occasions, that some insects after having their head removed live for up to 12 months. This may be due to instinctive reactions to light and other stimuli.

Five days after Putney Council received its eviction orders and four days after The Battle of Blackford's Path, Roehampton was still as calm as a corpse on diazepam. This was odd. Very odd.

One theory I had for the council's inaction, was that they were taking time mobilising a demolition team. After all, razing five tower blocks to the ground is a big operation. The complete non-appearance of the AB's was more difficult to explain. The gang had strong interests in Roehampton with a lot of money involved. Skag on the scale they were dealing it in was hugely profitable. Yes, the Roehampton team had suffered a setback from Four-wheel-drive and Ishmael, but that the AB's headmen could contemplate giving up such a fat nest as Roehampton was unthinkable. Blackford's Path would be answered. It was just a question of when and how.

As I looked down from my kitchen window, the wind raced a chaos of waste paper along Wanborough Drive and a Sainsbury's carrier bag flew high in the air like a kite. The temperature had dropped 10 degrees over the last three days. Winter had arrived, no-one could deny it. Then I caught a movement along the window ledge. It was just a blur but unmistakably a rat's tail. There was a sizable rat colony living in Witley Tower. These *Rattus norvegicus*, or brown rats, lived mostly in the basements and were big, red-eyed, lush-coated beauties. Most of the time they kept themselves to themselves, appearing only at night, so this daytime sighting was unusual. One reason for their shyness was that the building also supported a small but fierce colony of wild cats.

These ferals fed on scraps from the bins and on the rats, which they hunted in a pack. Occasionally, late at night, you would hear the cries of this pack as they surprized the foraging rats.

The phone rang. It was a man trying to sell five-gallon-sized drums of cooking oil. He suggested I take a couple of drums on a 'happy or return basis'. I could, if I liked, pay by standing order, there was a free gift (a pine soap dish) and he kindly consented to deliver the oil without a carriage charge. You have to admire these people, don't you? Getting up in the morning to go to work is traumatic enough, but getting up to try and cold-sell drums of cooking oil over the phone, is grim, hard work. Actually, I had another phone call that morning. It was from Kim.

'You haven't phoned, written, or anything,' she said.

'Kim, you've only been gone *two* weeks.'

'But you could have rung me. I've not gone to Jupiter, you know.'

Suddenly she began to cry. I'd never heard her cry before. It was a sound that I would have found hard to imagine.

'Oh, I suppose it's moving into the new house and every-thing, it's been fairly stressful and now things have settled down it's just come home to me that I don't live round the corner from my friends any more.'

'It's a different pace down there,' I said, in my kindest, most sympathetic-sounding voice. 'You'll get used to it …'

'I miss you,' Kim said.

'You miss *me?*'

'Yes.'

Now this was a remark which made me feel – although it's a contradiction – pleasantly uncomfortable. And for a second or two, I couldn't think what to say. So I warbled on about the people I missed in my life and ended up telling her about my Uncle Stu, who, one evening in the late sixties, went to a Pink Floyd concert at Parliament Hill Fields and never came back. Those old hippies – such style! But thinking of Stu made me feel sentimental and before I knew it, I'd agreed to go and visit Kim in Plymouth that very weekend. And do you know, all at once I was really looking forward to seeing her and I mean *really* looking forward. Ten minutes after the phone call, I was streaking towards the village in the chair – my mind blazing with all kinds of Kim-thoughts.

In the High Street, I pulled up outside the pet shop and went inside. Michael was sitting at the back of the shop, cuddling what looked like a lemur. There was one thing you couldn't fault Michael on, even though his zoological knowledge was not very strong, he did look after his animals. I knew of many instances where he'd refused to sell to people who he thought might be bad owners and he wouldn't hesitate to call in a costly vet to a sick animal.

'Michael, how are things?'

'Fine … I was only thinking about you yesterday – that you hadn't been in for a while.'

I was flabbergasted – a sentence of almost twenty words!

'How long have you had the lemur?'

'Two days.'

The ring-tail lemur that Michael was holding was the size of a domestic cat, had huge eyes, triangular ears, thick, soft black fur and a long white ringed tail. Lemurs are from Madagascar and are unusual enough to be expensive to import.

'Will you sell her?'

'No, I think I'll keep this one.'

I then asked Michael whether my yellow wolf spider had arrived. And sure enough, the spider was waiting for me. So I crossed my fingers and took a deep breath.

'Michael,' I said, 'you don't fancy a swap with a few sea horses, by any chance?'

Now this was a long shot, yet necessary as I was stony. I'd suggested specimen swaps in the past, but so far Michael had never agreed to one.

'If you like,' he said.

'Pardon?'

'I said, if you like.'

I couldn't believe it! Michael was actually agreeing to a swap! I put it down to the lemur and before it shat in his lap, or bit his nose, I grabbed my spider and skedaddled.

Spiders don't travel well, as they are delicate creatures with extremely high metabolic rates and often die of stress en route, particularly if they're being transported a long distance. Yet to my surprise, when I got this one home, he began feeding straight away. I was pleased, because it was a sign that he was in reasonably good shape. Then I took a chance. I know I shouldn't have. But after he'd eaten, I put him in with Clarissa.

Clarissa was my sole surviving yellow wolf spider. I'd had her longer than nearly any other arachnid and had bred from her on three or four occasions. At that time, I was desperate for wolf spiders, as I was running a detailed programme on them in The Happy Room, which had been interrupted by the cock-up with the poisonous arrow lizards.

Well, as soon as I dropped him in her tank, bold and cocky as you like, the young male immediately approached the older female. This was going to be interesting, I thought. He had to be cautious, though, as Clarissa was twice his size and quite capable of killing him should she feel so inclined. But a few centimetres from the big female the younger spider paused. Then, gently, he began to stitch his legs with hers. This was a clever tactic, as Clarissa seemed to quite enjoy it. Then the male took the situation by the mandibles, as it were, and swung onto the female's back. I thought he had moved too fast here and fully expected her to shake him off. But not a bit of it. She just sat there. For some reason, she'd taken a real shine to this young blood. Soon the male was dabbing at her underside and as if she'd been waiting for this, Clarissa's abdomen slid smoothly open and suddenly the two spiders were geometric with silks and flosses.

I was hopping with happiness. The gestation period of a wolf spider is about seven days. I just couldn't wait for the patter of hundreds of tiny feet.

25. Poetry Please

Random Thoughts And Themes – food that I like. Anything Chinese. Anything Indian. A doorstep of bread and butter. Black cherry yoghurt. Pizza with baked beans on top. Daddies sauce with anything.

Thursday was drop-in day at the centre. It was the only time – apart from The Chair Club – that I used the place, because I have an aversion to institutions of any sort. Not that the centre was particularly institutionalised, but I was wary all the same.

That day it was full and noisy – some were playing table tennis or pool, others chatted, or just sat staring into space. I wheeled to the end of the room and into the crèche. On Thursdays the crèche played social space to the centre's poetry group.

Now this group wasn't what you might call a serious poetry group. It was just a bunch of friends getting together for an hour or so for a natter. Though most weeks we did get around to reading a bit of poetry.

Lucy, Ishmael and Lenny had already arrived and Ishmael had just read one of his poems. This sounded like a quality piece, so I persuaded him to read it a second time, which, frankly, didn't take much doing. It went like this –

MY BEAUTIFUL HAMS

The sun tattoos a short story onto my arse
the story is well written, polemical and exciting,

110

so I offer my body up for more sunny transfers
and the hot scorchy process begins.
I become a sun vassal
a cipher for le soleil brille.

This is quite an event.
Soon my dorsal region is taken up by a publisher
sent to the British Library six times
given an ISBN number and published.
My sit-me-down becomes a good read!
We give lectures and recitals
appear on the radio
receive an honorary degree from a university
there's even talk of a TV series.
I say – it's good to have a crack that's famous –
a rose that's à la mode

My beautiful hams!

We clapped Ishmael. Which was unnecessary, but we did it anyway. And then I suggested that the poem would be an excellent candidate for the anthology. Everyone thought this was a sound idea and began to gab about the anthology.

Every year, the group received funding from a local health trust to produce a book of its work. And this was usually quite a reasonable read. We'd launch it at a public reading, or sometimes a series of readings and then for a month or two, hawk it around the local pubs and cafés. This was always good for a laugh. I remember one year, when we were out selling, we met another poetry group – Attack Poets. They were from somewhere up near Perivale and claimed to want to revive the oral traditions of poetry. One of their strategies, they explained, consisted of rushing into a pub, screaming a poem in unison at the startled customers, then rushing out again. It sounded a bit off the wall to me, but they were friendly enough and bought us drinks, so had my vote.

Next I read one of my short stories. I don't write stories often as I find poetry more satisfying. Yet so much was going on on the estate at that time that I felt I should put it down somehow and a diary seemed a bit old hat, so every once in a while, I would have a go at a short story.

The story I read that day was called *White Rat*. It was about a woman finding a half-dead white rat in Bessborough Road and wondering what to do with it. Eventually, after much debate with neighbours, she decides to take it to the vet. Very basic stuff really. When I'd finished reading *White Rat* Lucy and Ishmael clapped me, which was uncalled for because the story wasn't that good. I say Lucy and Ishmael clapped me, because Lenny didn't, and we soon found out why.

'It's rubbish …' he said.

I was afraid of this. Sometimes Len could get a bit excited in the group, which most of the time I put down to him forgetting to take his medication.

'Oh, Lenny, be positive,' said Lucy.

'I'm being positive. The story's crap, I don't believe a word of it.'

'Why?' said Ishmael.

'Who keeps white rats on the estate? No-one. They just don't exist as far as The Alton is concerned.'

'Lenny, someone *could* keep a white rat on the estate,' said Lucy. 'It's possible.'

'Well,' continued Lenny, 'if a tame white rat did escape, its instinct would be to go to ground, because if it hung around it would be quickly killed by wild rats, or a cat or dog. So on the reality scale, the story's piss poor …'

'But suppose this one had only been free for just a few minutes,' said Lucy, 'before the woman found it?'

'Yeah,' said Ishmael, 'its death by cats/dogs, whatever, is seconds from its escape, with the woman in between.'

'But why should it run into the road?' Lenny protested. 'Animals aren't stupid. Particularly rats. Why do you think they're used in so much scientific research? Because they're bright. No, if a domesticated animal like a white rat escaped, it would run up a tree or more likely, run down a hole, as I said.'

We left it there, me thinking that Lenny might just have a point for once. Funnily enough, he was next to read. He unravelled a sheaf of papers and gave everyone a copy of a poem.

'I've read this a few times in the group,' he said, 'for the last five meetings, actually. I hope you're not getting too bored with it?'

Silence greeted this, but Lenny had the hide of an rhinoceros, so he continued regardless –

YOU, EDEN, AND THE APPLE

You say you cannot see what is there –
recognise the obvious
that which is plain.

You say that Eden is not what you recognise –
that is plain. But did the apple have to know?
Did the apple have to know?
And the sky darkens us now
with immense gun-shaped clouds.

Again there was silence. Silence is a language that every poetry group is familiar with – if there is too much of it after you've read, then you take it that your piece hasn't gone down too well.

'Hmm,' I said, finally, 'quite a reasonable rhythm, I think.'

'But it could do with some work,' said Ishmael. 'Maybe another verse. Either way I don't think it's one of your best.'

Without warning, Lenny flung himself at Ishmael. Lucy and I were rooted to our seats, but Ishmael didn't flinch. He simply slapped Lenny's head hard with the palm of his hand as it arrived and Len flipped backwards, caught his shoulder on a table full of the crèche's toys and a large

113

white fluffy monkey fell on top of him. For a moment, monkey and poet wrestled. Then we all went bananas. I laughed, shrieking uncontrollably. Lucy laughed until tears were pouring down her face. And Ishmael just sat there grinning so widely that I thought he was going to split his head open.

26. Facts II

Random Thoughts And Themes – things that have gone out of fashion but still stick in my mind. Bovril. Capstan full-strength cigs. Sidecars for motorbikes. Sideburns for faces.

It's a fact that if the population of Earth continues to increase at its present rate, which is three thousand births a minute, by AD 3530, the total mass of human flesh and blood will equal the total mass of the Earth.

As I said earlier, I like facts, that's why I like history, but I like history not just for its people-related facts, which are absorbing, but because of the way history is linked with Nature. For I firmly believe history is recorded via a chronology almost all of which is Nature's. So it's surprising to me how so few historians study Nature. Perhaps if they did, they would conclude, as I have, that history is not just a record of human endeavour, but a record of the parallel development of Nature.

I would think a lot about this sort of thing when I was lying flat on my back in hospital, after the accident. Well, there wasn't much else to do. Now to get it out of the way, I may as well tell you about the accident, the little I remember, that is, for what I do recall is a strange lasso of memory.

My mother, Evangeline and I were driving to Kingston one Saturday morning in our 2CV. It was a warm, sunny day, I remember that very clearly. We were just passing Kings Mere Pond, which looked like a huge silver plate in the morning light, when Eva said she wanted to go to Syria to visit what's thought to be the site of the Garden of Eden.

'It's amazing,' she said, 'apparently you can still see some of the walls and bits of petrified wood and things ...'

'But that's all just legend,' I said.

'You want tablets of authenticity, I suppose?'

'Come on, Eva, it'll just be a few stones, with a little man standing at the gate selling camel-skin slippers and Palestinian scarves. Hardly worth the effort really.'

'How far from Damascus is it?' said my mother.

'About seventy miles,' said Eva.

'No, hang on,' I said, 'not slippers or scarves – ceramic apples and snakes with maybe a bit of hash cake thrown in ...'

'They say Damascus is a very lovely city,' said my mother.

'Some superb buildings ...' said Eva, 'and a very safe place to visit, apparently ...'

And they were the last words Eva and my mother ever spoke, for then came a sound that I can only describe as a metal yowl, followed by a great tail of glittering sparks. The next thing I remember was waking up in hospital with pneumatic drill-like pains pounding in my head and back.

It was about two weeks later that I found out exactly what had happened. We were hit by an forty-ton articulated lorry that was travelling at 65mph in a built-up area. My sister and I were thrown out of the car, which was then crushed virtually flat by the lorry. It's hardly necessary to add that my mother died instantly, but I don't like to forget it, because it's a small comfort. At least she didn't suffer.

When I finally left hospital, I wasn't very mobile. In fact I was completely helpless. But everyone in the block helped out. Hillary cooked my meals, Eileen Dear washed my clothes and Vile looked after my animals.

There is no way that you can explain what it's like, having your life and everyone you love suddenly smashed to pieces like that, or describe the loneliness that envelops you.

I wasn't on my own, of course, as Evangeline was still alive. If you could call it that. She was breathing, put it that way. Though at the beginning of my time in hospital, I couldn't quite get my brain around what had happened to her. It was only later when the full extent of PVS was explained to me that I began to understand. But life goes on, which is a shite expression, because unless you've got something worth living for, life doesn't go on. Yet with the help of my friends it did. Yes, I mustn't forget my friends! With their support I was soon getting out and about. But I quickly realised that getting out and about was almost as bad as staying in, for no matter where I went I saw my mother – in crowded streets, shops, on buses. It was very upsetting. So I stopped going out. I stopped doing anything that might remind me of her and it worked, almost. But the nights were the worst – not being able to sleep for thinking. Though I was lucky in a way, for because of my injuries, I was prescribed sleeping pills and trannies. So when things got too speedy, I popped a trannie and chased it down with a sleeping pill, which put me down nicely. But as time passed I simply got bored staying in and began to venture out once more – Richmond Park with Hillary and Francine, the common with Vile and Claire, gradually, things got better.

However, one afternoon, about eight months after the accident, while shopping in Safeways, a woman, a total stranger, approached me.

'You've had a loss?' she said.

'Sorry?'

'You've had a loss, haven't you?' repeated the woman.

She was in her early sixties, had deep-set eyes, crinkly lips and gave me a card – *Mrs T. Howell, Spiritualist*. I thanked her, put the card in my pocket and instantly forgot about it. But a week later, I mentioned the woman to Hillary and showed her the card. She was adamant that I should go and see Mrs T. Howell.

'If nothing else it will be an experience.'

'But what's the point?'

'There may not be one. It's just interesting …'

So Hillary and I went to see Mrs T. Howell (I was damned if I was going on my own). And I have to say it was all very comfy and down to earth. Mrs Howell made us very welcome in her small Sheen flat, where we sat in a sitting room crammed with Holman Hunt reproductions, nests of coffee tables and armchairs draped with antimacassars. There we had a cup of tea and a slice of Swiss roll.

A few minutes into my second slice of swiss roll (ever had swiss roll with custard? Honestly, it's as good as full sex) Mrs Howell put her cup down, closed her eyes and went into a sort of light trance –

'Here she is … she was waiting … a smallish woman with grey hair … now she's speaking … she says, stop grieving … it's time for you to stop grieving …'

Mrs Howell told me lots and lots of things about my mother and incredibly they were all, without exception, completely untrue. For example, my mother was not a 'smallish woman with grey hair'. She was tall with dark coloured hair. Nor was her home 'the countryside and the farm …' My mother was born in and lived all her life in the city. But I must admit, as I was sitting there in that neat little sitting room, I wished that what Mrs Howell was saying could be true. I really did.

At home, that evening, Hillary and I had a look through my old photo albums. There seemed to be more photographs of me than anyone, but being the first child I suppose that's only natural. There were also some photos of my father, which I didn't recall. I stared hard at these. Now my mother brought Evangeline and me up alone, because my father, a teacher, ran away with another teacher at about the time Eva was born. He then went to live in the United States, where by all accounts he continued his career as a running away from it person, until finally his heart took offence and attacked him. It was all the same to me. When he died, I felt nothing. To me, looking at photos of him as I did then, he was just a half-remembered, misty moustache.

Then I came to a section in the album called *The Marmoset*. This was full of snaps of a pretty little golden marmoset called Cilla.

27. Cilla

Random Thoughts And Themes – clothes that I remember. Very wide leather belts. Boys plaiting their hair. Velvet jackets. Jeans that had to be worn in the bath.

After the mysterious disappearance of Hammy, my striped hamster, whom I later reinvented as a cigarette card, my mother calmed the situation by buying me a pygmy marmoset.

Pygmy marmosets come from South America and are quite the dinkiest creatures you can imagine. They look like monkeys, but never grow more than 5 inches tall.

Cilla was blessed with a very cheeky character and at the slightest opportunity would run down your trousers, or up your skirt. She had a habit of instantly adopting people or things and once took a shine to one of Eva's toy bears. This toy was about three times larger than herself, yet last thing each night, the marmoset would insist on squeezing it into her cage.

As I'd done with Hammy, I quickly became besotted with Cilla and would race home from school every day to play with her. Then at bedtime, with the lights out, the antics would continue, as the tiny creature chased the beam of my torch around the skirting board. This went on for about six weeks, until one Saturday morning, I came home from running an errand to find Cilla lying still at the bottom of her cage.

'Cilla looks funny!' I cried.

'Don't shout, please,' said my mother, who was baking angel cakes in the kitchen.

'But she looks odd,' I protested.

'How do you mean, *odd*?'

'She isn't breathing.'

In my bedroom, my mother opened the marmoset's cage and gently lifted Cilla out.

'Is she dead?' I asked.

Without answering, my mother took the animal through to the kitchen and laid it on the table beside the angel cakes. It was then that I noticed that Cilla's fur was moulting.

'Her fur is falling off,' I said, astonished.

'Don't worry about that, that's normal.'

But it didn't look normal to me. I began to rummage in the pedal bin.

'We'll bury her in this,' I said, holding up an empty can of Italian chopped tomatoes. I could already imagine the funeral scene quite clearly. But my mother ignored me.

'Since the boiler house has shut down, the flat's been quite cool,' she said thoughtfully, 'bring me some tinfoil from the pantry, please.'

I went to the pantry and took out the roll of tinfoil.

'Pull off a piece about a foot square.'

As I did this, my mother turned on the grill of the gas cooker and with soft popping noises, the row of blue flames appeared.

'You're not going to cook her, are you?' I said.

'Do I look capable of cooking a marmoset?'

I wasn't sure about this, particularly as my mother then proceeded to wrap Cilla carefully in the tinfoil and lay her on the grill tray. She turned the gas of the grill down to very low and carefully placed the tiny animal underneath the flames.

'What are you doing?' I said.

'I'm not quite sure,' replied my mother.

As we watched, the tinfoil slowly began to unfold with the heat and then incredibly one of the marmoset's legs moved.

'DID YOU SEE THAT!!' I yelled.

'It could have been a nerve,' said my mother.

But then two legs twitched together and the marmoset opened an eye.

'SHE'S MOVING! SHE'S MOVING!' I screamed.

28. Laundry-a-go-go

Random Thoughts And Themes – what I'm ashamed of. My bent nose. My bent legs. My cruel thoughts.

It was time to wash some clothes. This instinct surfaced in me about three times a year.

There were two launderettes in the village. I always chose the one adjacent to The Montague pub, which was the cheaper of the two and had all of its windows boarded up, which reminded me vaguely of Witley Tower, so felt more homely. It was also where Deklon worked, who was the launderette's supervisor and another good friend of mine. Whenever I visited we would sit and have a good jaw. But why this particular visit sticks in my mind is because it was then that Dek told me about his flasher. This was not the Alton Estate's The Cape (community to community there are some things you share but your flasher isn't one of them). No, apparently The Jogger had come into the launderette on several occasions, each time dressed in a tracksuit and trainers. He'd seemed friendly enough, so at first had been welcomed. But on his third visit, while Deklon was busy sorting some service washes, the man flipped his tiny cock and balls out by the spin dryers and sent two women screaming into the street.

'I didn't know whether to hit him over the head with my mop, or call the police,' said Deklon.

This then developed into a sort of game. Every time Dek turned his back, The Jogger slipped into the launderette and exposed himself and ran out again. Eventually, they had him sectioned into the local psychiatric hospital, which pleased Dek, yet saddened most of his customers, as they thought the carry-on better than daytime TV.

After doing my washing, which took the best part of two hours, I got my finger out, as Wednesday was Evangeline's physiotherapy day.

29. Evangeline

*Random Thoughts And Themes – music that has played a signifi-
cant part in my life. Every Beatles track that I've ever heard (that's
the lot). Most Happy Mondays and Stone Roses' stuff. A song
written by my friend Paul Bowyer who lived not 50 yards from
Witley in Wanborough Drive.*

Warm sunlight spangled through the blinds across her face
and rippled the length of her body. I think I've mentioned
that a lot of PVS patients after a year or so move themselves
into a fetal position with their hands and feet curving
inwards. But not Eva. That's another reason why I knew she
would return to me one day. Plus the fact that she looked
so incredibly well. Okay, she was in a deep coma, but her
skin was still smooth and white, not flaky and blotchy like
the others. Moreover, her lips were moist, not cracked or
slimy. And finally, her hair was shiny and soft, not mousey
and full of split ends. All things considered, it didn't take
much to imagine her opening her eyes, sitting up and
saying hello.

But even though her body was supple and un-wasted,
after brain injuries of the sort that she had suffered,
muscles and limbs do stiffen, so physiotherapy, despite her
unconsciousness, was vital.

I fetched a trolley from reception and pushed it slowly
down to the ward. In her room, I slid the trolley alongside
the bed and carefully disconnected the feeding tubes.

Inside the hospital gym, Claudia, Eva's physiotherapist,
took hold of one of Eva's hands and squeezed it several

times. Claudia tested for responses all the time, even at this stage. It was exactly the right attitude for PVS, as you can never give up. That day we had quite a long chat about Evangeline's skin care. This was typical, since Claudia and I always discussed my sister in a very detailed fashion – teeth, hair, nails, skin, etc. This sort of dialogue was functional for my sister as well as being psychologically very useful for me. Which is another important PVS attitude.

Twenty minutes later, we lifted Evangeline gently into a canvas stretch frame and began the first serious exercises. This device was reminiscent of something mediaeval, for when my sister was strapped into it, she was suspended with virtually every part of her body held fast in elasticated straps. Then we carefully pulled at her limbs, via the straps, so exercising her major muscles.

After fifteen minutes of the stretch frame, we took her down, changed her into a costume and went through to the swimming pool. There I put her in line for the cradle hoist and hopped down to the changing room to get into my trunks.

In the pool, as I took Eva into my arms her hair fanned out across the surface of the water in a great arc and her thin white limbs spread. Sometimes her face would register a scowl or a quick grin, linking, doubtless, with thoughts that she was having deep down. But there in the pool it would always remain expressionless. I can't be sure, but I think she loved these swims. It pleased her physically, I know that, for her body always seemed to relax in the warm water, tendons and muscles loosening.

Presently, I would go through a series of movements with her which were again designed to tease her body into action. The idea being that it was safer to manipulate the muscles more rigorously when the weight of the body was supported by water.

After about twenty minutes of this, Eva was hoisted out once more and I had a quick swim.

When I came out of the changing room at about four o'clock Four-wheel-drive, who was the swimming pool tech, was kneeling on his sticks beside the water, filling test tubes.

'Had a good one?' he said.

'Not bad. Now I fancy a nice cup of tea.'

Cups were rattling all over the hospital. When I'd taken Eva back to the ward and settled her, I caught the goods lift down to the basement. There, in amongst the boilers and filtering equipment, Four-wheel-drive had a bench space for his pH tests and an electric kettle. With a mug of steaming tea each, we took the goods lift back up to the roof where it was quiet.

We sat beside the massive Victorian chimneys, sipping our tea and looking down at the traffic whirling 100ft below.

'We've lost the summer now,' said Four-wheel-drive.

'It's getting colder all the time,' I agreed.

'You know, if it didn't get cold in winter, it wouldn't be so bad.'

'What, hot snow and warm icicles?'

'At least that would be more cheerful. The cold's a pisser.'

Then beyond the car fumes and the reek of the city, I smelled fresh cut grass. Four-wheel smelled it too. We stared steadily into the slowly gathering dark, straining to see where that wonderful smell was coming from.

30. Siobhán

Random Thoughts And Themes – tower blocks. I was born in a tower block, so I've watched them for years. Now they are even in the mountains: in the South of France, on the edge of Marseilles, they march into the countryside until they stand inside the Someio range. I imagine waking in one of those lofty apartments, my head literally in the clouds. There I drift slowly to the soft rhythms of the taut steel piling humming gently in the warm brick and am happy.

When I took Eva swimming on Wednesdays, it reminded me of Siobhán. Siobhán had been an excellent swimmer and was my second girlfriend.

As well as being a good swimmer she was also a good gymnast. I was into sport at school too, mainly fives and cricket, so we often stayed behind together for after-school training.

We would be hooting and laughing all the time, particularly in the changing rooms, because if it was just the two of us, we'd change and shower together. Though the last time we did that was strange.

It was a rainy Thursday in May, but early May, so it wasn't too warm. As a result, only three of us had stayed behind that evening – Siobhán, Jim Robertson and me.

Jim Robertson was in the school squash and fives teams, but for some reason, had allowed himself to be persuaded by the Head of PE to take up the javelin as well. Jim hated it and was getting angrier and angrier by the day. Siobhán and I hung out of the changing room windows and watched him practise on the javelin pitch. With a scowl Jim balanced the alloy spear carefully in one hand, then blowing like a cross bull, began the run-up. But at the last moment, just before the throw, slipped and fell on his bum. Siobhán and I nearly damaged ourselves laughing.

'Jim, it's the way you throw 'em!' yelled Siobhán.

'Just one more time, please!' I begged.

He lifted himself to his feet, turned to us and swore. Then Siobhán did something wonderful – she stepped down from the window and peeled her sweatshirt and vest off in one go. I stared at her heavy breasts.

'You're lovely …' I said.

'Actually,' said Siobhán, 'I've got one nipple larger than the other. Look …'

And with that she took her left breast in her hand and gently squeezed the nipple. But I couldn't tell the difference – the two of them looked spot on to me. Then I took the situation by the collar as it were.

'Now look, we're still going out, aren't we?'

Siobhán pulled a face.

'Sort of, but I'm really busy at the moment.'

'You're dumping me!'

'I'm not dumping you! But I must concentrate on work right now. And what about you? You're in exactly the same boat.'

This time I pulled a face.

'Yeah, but what are you doing Friday night?'

'I've just told you – studying.'

We finished changing in a loud poetry group-type silence. She was right about the work, though, it really was catching up on us. Exams had never bothered me much, but we'd been let down by our GCSE history and economics teachers, who had changed twice in a term, which had left us behind on both syllabus targets.

At the pool gate, I had trouble with the lock. It was always stiff, but that evening was even slightly rusty.

'Shall I have a go?' said Siobhán.

The lock immediately snapped open.

'I think I can manage,' I said, tonelessly.

The pool was open-air, unheated, and sometimes none

too clean. That evening leaves, a newspaper and a dead cat floated in the still water.

'Look at that!?!' said Siobhán, pointing at the cat.

'Shit, I'm not going in there,' I said.

'It's only a cat.'

'Yeah, but it's dead.'

Siobhán knelt at the pool side, stretched an arm out and began to paddle the water. I stared down at her. The slender curve of her back was covered in an Artex of swirling freckles. Instantly, I got an erection. The trouble with this woman was that she was attractive from any angle. Siobhán reached the dead cat, yanked it out by its tail and flung it at me. I jumped back. But I was moving far too slowly as the icy corpse slapped hard across my chest.

'YOU BASTARD!'

'Cat is really good for you,' laughed Siobhán, 'meat's incredibly lean.'

'I'm soaked!'

'Not going to matter too much when you get in, is it?'

'Siobhán, why have you thrown a dead cat at me?'

'Damn! I've forgotten my goggles.'

Siobhán danced back out of the pool gate and ran back towards the PE block. I wiped my chest with my towel and stared down at the cat. He must have slipped into the pool during the night and drowned when he couldn't get out. Perhaps he was chasing something, or maybe something was chasing him. He was large, black and white and had his eyes open, which I didn't like. It's not true that people and animals die with their eyes closed. In fact it's almost impossible, as the halting of the blood flow at death quickly contracts the obucularis muscles, forcing the lids open. I gave the body a nudge with my foot. It felt hard, like a lump of wood. Dead things always feel like that, don't they? Death is solid. Ungiving. Whereas Life is always soft. Spongy.

'Introduced yourself?' said Siobhán, returning.

'Yes, his name's Woody and his hobbies are reading and cycling.'

'Remember, no tongues first date …'

Siobhán slipped her goggles over her face and then did a perfect swallow dive into the water. With a kick like an outboard motor, she then front-crawled to the opposite end of the pool, turned and began the butterfly back. Here I was reminded of a ship's figurehead, its torso ploughing through the waves. Again, I couldn't keep my eyes off her breasts. I know this is a bit classic – ogling a women in a swimming costume. But Siohbán's breasts were quivering with the motion of her swivelling arms in a way that I'd never seen before. Predictably, I got another erection. You can see the problem. I was mad about a woman who didn't give a toss for me. Of course, that was a grave mistake on her part. I was the attentive, amusing, kind, unselfish lover who was totally right for her. That was obvious. But why did she not see this? Yes, all Siobhán had to do was snap her fingers and there I was, a jibbering, salivating idiot. It was pathetic. And that was the real problem – my desire for her was up in neon. She could hear it, smell it, taste it, it was fountaining from me. And that's unattractive, isn't it? How can anyone love a human being that's become a dog? Dogs are to be patted, taken for walks, you don't have an affair with one.

After our swim we showered together but significantly still wearing our costumes. And that was the last time we did that, costumes or not.

31. The Happy Room

Random Thoughts And Themes – body hair. In ancient Britain, hairlessness was a highly fashionable condition, as the Roman general Trebonius discovered in 46 BC upon examining the corpse of the Cassi Chief, Caswallon, for the Briton had had every single one of his body hairs removed.

At home, after dinner, as the insect arena was a mess, I went through to The Happy Room and had a bit of a clean-up. I'd been pitting yellow scorpions against poisonous giant centipedes, with the result that the scorpions had run riot and scissored the centipedes to pieces. Which was disappointing. But as I looked across to the water arena, I was more pleased: the pike and goldfish were still the best of friends.

The Happy Room was the sharp end of my behavioural experiments at Witley. Yes, in my tiny lab, in that semi-derelict tower block, something very special was happening: a series of experiments that theoretically could affect the behavioural characteristics of every creature known to science.

Now this was an ambitious programme. Which I've avoided telling you about until now, because I wanted you to get to know me and my lifestyle of that time. For then, hopefully, you'd be able to understand the nature of the work, as I'm aware that anyone giving The Happy Room a quick look, or coming to it without preparation, could easily walk away with a very wrong impression.

Yes, my Happy Room programme had involved the participation of over four hundred individual animals and nearly fifty species. But before I tell you all about it, I'm going to have to give you a short introduction into Gene Origin Theory. Sorry about this, I'll keep it as brief as possible. Promise.

The human body is a very strange brew indeed. For it contains a near perfect mixture of sodium, potassium, chloride, cobalt, magnesium and zinc that once existed in the primordial sea. So inside us laps and flows a marine cocktail almost as old as the planet itself. But this is not a coincidence. It's part of the order of things. We are Nature. Nature is us. Us being the Earth and every single living thing on it, where all Life is inter-related via the same basic carbon molecular structure and DNA source material. So the bacterium is the orchid, the orchid is the salmon, the salmon the swallow, the swallow the panther and so on.

Now here comes the tricky part. We know that almost all of the known universe is in chaos. In fact the only part of it that is not in chaos is the part that has Life. For Life is not and can never be chaotic, as it's a cause and effect system. In other words, its very essence is Order. Without Order, Life simply cannot be sustained. But Life is not plentiful in the universe. At the moment, the only place that we know has Life is this planet. It therefore follows that the Earth is the only known source of Order in the universe. So -

Life = Order = Earth

Although there are many things that science can predict on this planet, there are many things that it cannot. The main problem being that scientists only understand the substance of roughly half the Laws of Nature, this is the intention of all science – to understand and control Nature, through a working knowledge of its laws. But although there are lots of things in Life that we do understand, there is only one certainty for us and that is Death. Back to Death again!

But Death is a most vital component of the life cycle, beyond even Birth. For it is Death that makes sure that fresh genes are always prominent. This is done by making the old genes defunct, via the host body dying. So Life is continually building up gene patterning in species that are ever stronger, containing ever more knowledgeable source material. This is a crucial biological performance, so much so that many scientists believe that an organism's main function is gene replication. Consequently -

Life = Order = Earth = The Gene Machine

It's my belief that all creatures have complex genetic patterning of matriarchal and patriarchal mechanisms that bind us to each other, even between species. These mechanisms have very real psycho-genetic components without which no species could possibly cope with the strain of existence. They'd simply die from the stress of living, Life being the fiercest stimulus of all. And here's where I come in. What's the best way of producing the most potent and data-smart genes? Why, by providing happy, healthy, stress-free bodies for them to exist in, of course. So what's the true road to producing happy, healthy bodies? Undeniably – peace amongst species. But what thwarts this is the component of aggression in species. So if aggression could be eradicated from animals, then Life could only evolve more efficiently.

Yet to combat a creature's aggressive behaviour is not easy. The world is a tough place, Darwin's Theory of Evolution with its survival of the fittest dynamics, is still the testament of species, with the exception of man (although that's debatable). But just think what could be achieved if aggressive behaviour in animals could be efficiently controlled. The gene replication process would be facilitated many times over. But just *how* can aggressive behaviour be effectively taken out of a species' psycho-genetic profile?

I believe the key is to take away the stress of living. When that is managed the whole scale of animal behaviour is open to adjustment. For instance, I once saw a cat mauling a squirrel. In the fight, the cat tore one of the squirrel's legs off. So I captured them both and when the squirrel was well, evened things up a bit – I fastened the cat's legs together, wired his mouth shut and then gave him to Three Legs (the squirrel).

The squirrel didn't do much, just gave the cat a nip or two. But guess what? From then on that cat had a healthy respect for squirrels. I'm telling you, I was breeding praying mantises that fed on berries, snakes that ate fruit, and spiders that stalked nothing more sinister than a saucer of milk. It can be done. The biogenetic life cycle is not impregnable. Nature's mechanisms *can* be reset. Yes, I know it's a massive project, that'll take ages, but everything, no matter how huge or complex, has to begin somewhere. And what is so worthwhile here is that the prizes are so enormous. Okay, that's enough theory for now. But later we may have to say hello to micro-genetics, we'll see how things go.

Just before I went to bed that evening, I got the reptile arena ready for the morning. I was going to put an African black-headed viper in with a rat. If the rat was killed in say, five minutes, I would leave the next one in for four minutes and so on, until the viper began to get the idea that he was never going to kill a rat again. Then in would go the yoghurt and prunes. You know, the story really is never-ending.

32. Cafe´ Delight

Random Thoughts And Themes – plants and planets. The planet Earth with all its carbon forms and communications impedimenta has much the same shape and patterning as the human brain with all its fleshy systems and structuring. Weird or what?

Early the following day at about 8am I called in at the Double Bubble. The café was full and Maurice was busy, but as I sat down at my table, I could tell that he wanted to talk to me about something.

'Hey, guess what?' he yelled from behind the counter, which was stacked with dirty plates and cutlery.

'Tell me,' I said.

'They're letting me change at Thames Valley. I'm going to do a research MA: *Prosthetics in Literature.*'

'Great!'

'Hippolyte's false leg in *Madame Bovary*, the Domo's plaster hand in *The Duchess of Malfi*, Pinocchio's wooden nose in ...'

At that moment the street door was nearly yanked off its hinges by a huge man in a filthy RAF greatcoat.

'What can I do for you?' said Maurice, instantly.

'A tea,' said the big man.

'Takeaway?'

'No, I'll drink it here.'

'I can do you a takeaway.'

'No, I'll drink it here.'

'Sorry, I can't do that.'

'Why not?'

'Because you're not clean enough.'

It was true. The man stank. His hands were shiny black, his hair was more woven than a hearth rug and there was something sticking to his arse that looked very much like a flattened turd. But he just turned on his heel, wrenched open the door again and disappeared into the street.

At this point I wondered whether I should buy a tea or not. And if I did, whether it should be small or large? I considered the determinants: the average small-sized cup of tea yields, on average, five average-sized mouthfuls. As opposed to the average large cup of tea (on average 17% more expensive) which yields about eight average-sized mouthfuls (differential 37.5%). I checked the bank. I had £2.49.

'Mo, give me a large tea, please.'

Fuck the determinants, I thought. The door opened again and in came Ishmael.

'You'll never guess?' he said.

'Go on,' I said.

'A man came into the studio this morning and wanted me to tattoo VISA on one arm and ACCESS on the other.'

'Honestly?'

'As I stand here.'

'But why?'

'His girlfriend fancied it.'

'Did she work for a credit card company, or something?'

'I don't know. I didn't ask.'

'Well, did you do it?'

'It's what he wanted.'

'Holy Christ, the whole world is a mental hospital!'

'What was I supposed to do? I have to pay the rent, you know.'

'True.'

'Egg, bacon, double bubble and two slices, Mo, please.'

'Eggs – flipped or unflipped?' said Maurice.

'Flipped.'

'Bacon – normal or crispy?'

'Crispy.'

'Bubble – moist or dry?'

'Moist.'

Ishmael sat down and we set up for a game of chess.

Maurice kept several chess sets to hand in the café as he had quite a keen bunch of chess-playing regulars. Ishmael and I were two of the keenest. As a matter of fact, so keen were we that we'd invented several café forms of the game.

Bitch Chess. This was played with only seven pieces – three queens either side and one neutral king in the middle of the board. The objective was the opposite of ordinary chess – to *uncheckmate* the king. Then there was Banzai Chess. This was played with two queens, two rooks and two captains either side. A captain being a new piece, modelled on a chain-mailed fist rising from a crenellated base, which moved one square forward and always moved. So, in effect, when it was your turn, you repositioned *two* pieces. There was no king, the object of the game being purely to attack.

We played a game of Bitch Chess, which was over in three minutes flat. I uncheckmated Ishmael's king seventeen times before he forced a draw.

'I've got three appointments this afternoon,' said Ishmael.

'Sounds as if business is picking up.'

'If it is, it's not before time.'

Initially, Ishmael ran his tattoo studio from the back of a mini van. But once the word spread about how good an artist he was, trade boomed and he was soon able to rent a basement shop a few doors along from the Double Bubble.

'So how's *The Project*?' I asked.

'Coming on …' said Ishmael. 'I had an hour on it this morning.'

The Project was Ishmael's master work. Though quite what it was, no-one could say, it was a secret. But just how do you keep a tattoo project secret, you might well ask? Surely the person you're tattooing has to know? Unless you're tattooing yourself, of course. But Ishmael had always said he'd never wear tattoos, so the exact nature of *The Project*, remained a mystery.

'By the way,' said Maurice, 'did you hear about the crash?'

'Crash?' I said.

'In King's Mere Pond on the common.'

'*In* King's Mere?'

'That's what I heard. A Daf pantechnicon swerved off the A3 and crashed right into it.'

'Casualties?'

'Two ducks, apparently … Dear Mr and Mrs Mallard, you ducked, missed the shit, but caught the van.'

33. To Further or Not to Father

Random Thoughts And Themes – the aesthetics of Nature. A blade of grass is beautiful, but so is the ugliest creature in the world – the vole-rat, particularly when one skins them, so exposing their artery and vein complexa.

At about 6pm that evening I got a surprise – it was Hillary shouting up to my window. She was lucky to catch me as I was just on my way out. But this was a flying visit, apparently. I sent the lift down and within minutes she was sitting on my sofa telling me something extraordinary.

'I'm pregnant.'

'What?'

'I'm pregnant.'

Now this I hadn't expected and for a moment, just a moment, I was winded, which, I'm embarrassed to say, showed a little.

'PREGNANT!?! BUT HOW FOR GODSAKE!?!'

'In the usual way, Dean, I think.'

'By *who*, I mean? Who's the father?'

'I'd rather not say.'

Swiftly I did a bloke-crunch through the people Hillary knew that I knew, but came up with sweet FA. There wasn't a steady or a flirt amongst the lot of them.

'Well, are you happy about it?' I said.

'Yes, I think so. Look, can you come over for lunch tomorrow, at about one?'

'Fine.'

'I'll tell you more then.'

And with that she was gone.

What was going on? Hillary had had a titanic struggle to keep things shipshape while bringing up Francine on her own, so was another child such a good idea? But maybe she was having a big romantic scene with someone? Though in that case, why hadn't she told me about it? It was all very curious.

Before I went out for the evening, I checked on The Happy Room. I had a fascinating trial going on. I was weaning three ferrets off fresh meat.

Firstly, I'd built a fairly realistic-looking rabbit out of a steel armature, some fur and chicken bones. Then I'd wired the armature with a 50 volt supply, placed it in the mammal arena and introduced the ferrets. Ferrets are, as is well known, vicious killers and will attack even cats and dogs. Predictably, they immediately attacked the pretend rabbit, but as they did so, received 50 volts for their trouble. They immediately gave the rabbit a wide berth. Though they came back after about fifteen minutes and went through the whole thing again. Which led me to conclude that ferrets may possess very short short-term memories. So in an attempt to stretch a point (and a short-term memory) I upped the voltage to 75v. And guess what? It worked! The ferrets became very rabbit-respectful after only one pass. If things continued like this, I thought, I'd try them with a live rabbit in the morning.

34. Night Ride

Random Thoughts And Themes – the poet and the penis. The poet Paul Eluard was said to have had a penis shaped like a tulip. One evening, after particularly ardent coition, his wife Gala observed that her husband's bulbous member was glowing crimson. Eluard immediately christened his organ – 'the stalk and flower of love'.

The common was very dark and the air had a stewy tang to it, so I switched on the chair's fog lamps and chewed each breath before I swallowed it. Then a line came to me –

> at dusk he starts his silent cruising ...

By the time I'd arrived at The Heath, I had two verses. I paused in reception to jot them down –

> at dusk he starts his silent cruising
> eyes bright as match-flame
> padding the new shadows of the dimming wood
>
> later, he begins the real work –
> moistening moss, inflating fungus
> unfettering the nightjar

It needed another two or three stanzas, but it was a start. Just as I was about to go down to the wards two middle-aged men, one wearing a dressing gown, came out of the lift and shuffled slowly towards the main doors. The Heath didn't have a casualty department, at night the reception area was shut, so sitting at the back as I was, I must have been almost invisible.

'I needed £8 million to buy …' said the man in the dressing gown, 'so I borrowed £6 million. Which cost me a £1 million. But I didn't put the £6 million down, instead I put £1 million down as a deposit, invested the rest and sub-let the property. In six months I made £1 million from the sub-let and £500,000 interest from the investment. Then I sold the property for 8½ million. So in half a year I'd made £1 million.'

'Fantastic!' said the man's companion. 'Fantastic!'

On the PVS ward it was very quiet. I mouthed a hello to Fiona, the night sister and went and sat with Evangeline.

Eva had loved the Russian poets. Her favourite was Gleb Gorbovsky. So that evening, I read her a few of his poems. And I quickly realised why she'd loved him so. His images were like hers, witty and wise, but also very romantic. I especially liked one poem called Sky, which was about two skies – one above the head, the other inside it.

That night I had a dream which in a way was very Eva-like. It started with a grinning Vile handing me a small, brightly coloured knapsack sporting a Zippy from *Rainbow* sticker. I unfastened the knapsack and inside was what looked like an ordinary builder's brick, but black in colour. I took the brick out. Sure enough, it was a black-coloured builder's brick. It even had the legend London Brick Company pressed into its V-shaped centre. But two things bothered me. One, it was not as heavy as I expected a builder's brick to be. And two, the colour wasn't right somehow. For the more I looked at it, the more I came to realise that it was not black-coloured at all, but a very dark green and it smelled like …

'Jesus!'

Vile laughed.

'How did you get it shaped like that?' I asked.

'Used a London Brick Company mould, how else?'

'Is it good stuff?'

'The very best.'

'Worth?'

'Cut into £25 deals – about eleven thousand.'

We started selling the blow brick on a street corner. Vile had cut it into neat slices which he'd then wrapped in the wings of tiny birds (remember, this is a dream).

A big man passed by wearing a plaid shirt and triple pigtails.

'Puff?' said Vile.

'What you got?' said the man, without hesitation.

'The best blow you'll ever know. Go on, spoil your lungs.'

The big man smiled. 'Let's see.'

Vile reached into the Zippy pack, took out one of the deals and a pair of tiny wings fluttered open to reveal the dark lozenge of cannabis.

'How much?' said the man, plainly impressed.

He decided on two deals and as Vile organised this, two smartly dressed Chinese boys appeared. At first they seemed to want to buy, yet as the big man left, one of them pulled out a knife.

'BASTARDS!!' yelled Vile, and kicked out at the knifeman.

The kick caught the boy perfectly under the chin and catapulted him backwards, but his sidekick promptly drew a handgun and at point-blank range shot Vile twice in the neck. The gunfire lit up the street like a photo session. And as the two boys sprinted away, Vile collapsed on the pavement.

'The Zippy,' choked Vile, 'don't let the cunts get the Zippy.'

Then a big black car drew up, a window slid down and the face of a woman emerged, but a face horribly injured – bloody flaps of flesh hung from her cheeks and a swath of dried blood glittered at her throat like a necklace.

'Lift?' she whispered.

'Go!' spluttered Vile. 'Go!'

I snatched the Zippy and then I was running. Running

anywhere. Running nowhere. I ran inside a nearby shop.

'Over here,' said a saleswoman, suddenly appearing, 'are all the wearables – rubber wear, plastic wear, edible wear. If it's *wear*, it's here.'

'What's edible wear?' I said, trembling.

'Clothes you can eat,' said the woman.

She picked up a pair of edible knickers that were neatly packed in a cellophane bag.

'These are quite popular. Taste a bit minty. There was a Malaysian company making edible sets at one time – bra/panties/tights. But they had a sell-by-date and had to be refrigerated. We just didn't have the space ...'

'How much?' I heard myself say.

The woman stabbed at a cash register, the drawer flew open, birds' wings flapped and fluttered.

'Cash or ornithology?' said the woman.

I fumbled through my clothes.

'Hold on a minute,' I said, 'I've got a couple of chaffinches somewhere ...'

35. One of Us is Missing?

Random Thoughts And Themes – Blackburn. Ever noticed how you never meet anyone that claims to come from Blackburn? It's also one of the few cities in the country that I've never had a reason to visit. Hmmm …

Noon the next day and police were crawling all over Witley. At first I thought the eviction had started, but as it turned out, Webley had gone missing.

'When was the last time you saw Mr Webley?' asked a detective.

There I was stuck. For the caretaker was such a skiver we didn't see him from one week to the next.

'I can't remember,' I said, truthfully, 'maybe five or six days ago?'

'Would you say he was a popular figure on the estate?'

For a second, just a second, I got an image of Webley wearing a gold lamé suit, crooning with mike to hundreds of adoring Alton Estate fans.

'No.'

'Why is that?'

How do you explain years of ill-temper and inefficiency? I gestured at the wreck of the building that was Witley and told him that once it was a grand Le Corbusier design. Now it was a ruin. There were quite a few people to blame for that and Webley was one of them.

At 12.30pm, I was breezing across the common again. I went via King's Mere Pond this time, to have a look at the crashed lorry. But there was nothing there, just a silent pond.

As Hillary opened her door warm cooking smells billowed out behind her. This made me think of the flying fish and for a second my stomach did a forward roll. I was waved inside and carefully threaded myself through stacks of cardboard boxes and bundles of clothes. In the kitchen I came across Eileen Dear sitting behind a huge mound of washing. I kissed her on the cheek and we began to chat. But something was bothering me.

'Hillary, tell me,' I said, 'what's that lovely smell?'

Eileen laughed and Hillary joined in. The odour was a meaty one, but with a sort of acute sweetness that I'd never come across before.

'It's a surprise,' said Hillary, 'something you'll recognise, I think.'

'Now I'll leave you two to it,' said Eileen, rising to go.

'You're not having lunch with us?' I said.

'Not today, I'm going to the hairdresser's.'

As Eileen passed down the hallway, broad beans and broccoli arrived on the kitchen table, plus a sizable braising dish. Inside this dish, lay two identical lumps of meat bubbling in a thick reservoir of reddish gravy.

'What is it?' I pleaded.

'Guinea pig,' said Hillary.

'Guinea pig?' I said quietly.

'Yes,' said Hillary, 'they're staple diet in Guyana, you know.'

After the meal, Hillary made coffee and I went and sat in the sitting room. Like everywhere else, this was also upside down. There were piles of Hillary's books and Francine's toys everywhere. And on a side table, blinked a familiar accessory – Hillary's Amstrad. I recognised the style immediately:

The astral body is a facsimile of our mental and physical existence. It is our physic double and can pass through any physical barrier, travelling virtually anywhere. This last point is particularly crucial in understanding the out of body experience: decide to travel

*and you travel, think that you journey by thought alone and you
instantly arrive ...*

I liked that last bit – *decide to travel and you travel, think that
you journey and you instantly arrive ...*

Hillary came in with coffee and biscuits.

'I'm sorry it's a bit cramped in here.'

'Stop apologising. You know my place looks like this all
the time. By the way, where are your mum and dad?'

'Mum's got an appointment at Queen Mary's for a
hearing test and Dad's gone with her. Did I tell you the
council have offered me a house in Purley?'

'Purley? They eat babies out there, you know.'

'My main problem is Francine – I don't want to move
her from school. Oh, I wish we were all back in Witley and
things were calm and peaceful again.'

There was a pause as we both considered this, then
Hillary reached down a jar of sugar from the top shelf of
the dresser and I realised it was true, she did look pregnant.
Not very pregnant, but pregnant enough to look pregnant,
if you know what I mean.

'So you're pregnant then?' I said, plunging straight in.

'Yes.'

'Well, tell me about it. Who is the father? I'm dying to
know.'

Hillary stared at me with an I'm-unsure-whether-to-trust-
you expression on her face.

'Only if you promise to keep it utterly to yourself.'

'Of course ... But I'm a little hurt you'd think I'd tell
anyone.'

'I know ... Well, I'm not sure whether you're going to
believe this, but in a way there is no father, although there
is biologically speaking. I've taken part in an artificial
insemination programme.'

'You did it with a bit of plastic!?!'

'Don't be horrible. No-one came along that I wanted to
have a child with. So ...'

'You shagged with a syringe.'

'I'll hit you over the head with my Amstrad in a minute.'

'Do you know the identity of the donor?'

'No, and I don't want to. I don't see that it's an issue. It may become one later on. If it does, I'll cope with it then.'

'Well, I don't know what to say.'

'How about congratulations?'

'Yes, sorry, congratulations. How pregnant are you?'

'Ten weeks … You know, last night I got up at 4am, fried some chips, smothered them in sugar and scoffed the lot.'

'Pregnancy craving?'

'Maybe, but I never did anything like that when I was carrying Francine.'

And as I looked at Hillary, I really could see her pushing a pram again.

'Can I be a godfather?'

'Dean, what a nice thought.'

On my way home, I passed by the centre and saw Bim in the playground. He'd been out of hospital a week and was sitting in his wheelchair gazing down at a piece of fluff dancing in a draught. This was typical Bim. As I approached he looked up and smiled. His face was a bit scabbed and battered, but otherwise he didn't look too bad. I flopped my arm around his shoulders and all at once, from behind, someone slid their hands over my eyes and Four-wheel-drive put on a disguised voice –

'Who is this man?' he said.

The hands were removed and I turned around.

'Where've you been? Haven't seen you down the club for ages,' said Four-wheel.

'The council are going to hit Witley soon, so we've had to be on our guard.'

'You know, when that war finally happens, I want to be there.'

'I should think that could be arranged.'

36. Fresher Days

Random Thoughts And Themes – attraction. People are attracted to members of the opposite sex who have a similar intelligence level and colouring, but most importantly, according to research, their middle finger has to be the same length as their own.

It had come around very fast, but I was due to start a degree in microbiology at Surrey University the following Monday.

I had applied to other universities, but Surrey seemed to be quite a bit friendlier than the rest. The friendly factor really counts nowadays in Higher Education, as you can easily find yourself locked into a three-year honours degree, with possibly a fourth year for a teaching cert/MA/MSc, whatever. So if the place isn't sociable, it could be a grind.

Another good thing about Surrey was that it had excellent wheelchair access. For me, that, the friendliness, and the fact it was fairly local – one bus ride along the A3 – were the deciding factors. Though going to college was not without its problems. For instance, what was I going to wear? And what would I carry my books in? Two serious worries. The first was quickly solved when I reasoned that since I owned only two pairs of jeans and three T-shirts, my dress options were fairly limited. The second was more tricky, but boiled down to a straight toss-up between three carrier bags: a white, strong-looking, no-nonsense Dewhurst Butchers' type; a green and gold, fancy, Harrods/Bentalls model; or a design-bereft, if-I'm-given-one-more-of-these-I'll-go-gaga Tesco's job. It was an exhausting brain teaser, but finally I went for the Dewhurst – its class credentials set it apart.

I then spent the rest of the week getting the two domestic hotspots in my life – Eva and the menagerie – primed for new schedules. I arranged for Claudia to change Eva's physiotherapy period from Wednesday morning to Friday morning, when I had a free period, and then introduced my animals to an earlier morning feed and a later evening feed, which they soon got used to. Then on the Saturday evening I got a surprize visit from Lenny –

'An acre of average farmed soil contains a ton of fungi, at least 2 tons of bacteria, 220 pounds of protozoa, 120 pounds of algae and nearly 100 pounds of yeasts. How do I know this?'

'You're doing an Open University course in soil erosion in your spare time?' I said.

'No.'

'Okay, it's some sort of self-learning thing.'

'Precisely, it's a self-learning thing ...'

'Oh, I see, this is a dig at me going to college.'

'What is 'an education' these days? A simple excuse for dossing around and partying.'

'Sounds good to me.'

'But what is the point of studying for years and not being able to get a job at the end of it?'

'What's the alternative, that's the real question? Besides, I need the proximity of other science folk. I need to kick my ideas around with some like-minded people.'

'Well, it sounds like a colossal waste of time.'

'Thanks for the encouragement, Len.'

On the Monday I got up at 6.30am.

As I saw it, the one major problem with my going to Surrey was the eviction orders. I didn't want to come home and find Witley a pile of rubble and my animals scattered to the four corners. So after I'd checked the traps and fed everyone, I nipped up to the sixth floor.

Again Vile's front door was wide open. This was not like

him at all. It was worrying. I went through to his bedroom and knocked on the door. But there was no answer. So I peeked in. Sure enough Vile was in bed, but he was not alone, for stretched beside him under the duvet, was Claire. That damned dog! Then I saw the framed photos. They were dotted all around the room and were all of the toza. She was bounding along in the park with a stick in her mouth. She was gazing straight into the camera with her tongue hanging out. She was lying on her back with her legs in the air. Now I'd always known that Vile was lonely, but up until then, I hadn't realised just how lonely. I gently shook him awake.

'THE BASTARDS!?!' he shouted, jackknifing up.

'No, no,' I said. 'Relax, everything's okay.'

I then explained my fears about going to college and we quickly agreed on an emergency procedure for getting word to me at Surrey, should and when the Alton Armageddon kick off. Then, with much passion, Vile told me about a new cocaine-lithium design he was working on. I had trouble stifling a yawn here, but was kind and did so.

My start at Surrey was 10.30am. So leaving myself plenty of time, which when travelling is always a good idea for the sensible para, I got out my sticks and made my way down to the village. I thought I would leave the chair at home for the first week or so – I'd hit them with the glitz trolley later.

You know, there's only one thing I hate more than a crowded bus and that's a crowded bus full of people who are soaking wet. For as I arrived at the bus-stop, it bucketed down with rain. I was only standing there for about three minutes, but that was enough, I got utterly soaked and so did everyone else in the queue. Then I had to sit for the entire forty-minute journey to Guildford with the stench of wet clothes wafting up my nose.

In all honesty, wet plastic, as in a plastic mac, is not an unpleasant smell. Neither is wet Gortex, as in a cagoule. Wet gaberdine, as in a raincoat, can be foul smelling, particularly if it's a dusty raincoat. But the worst wet-smell of all is wet wool. Wool absorbs every kind of smell lovingly. And sitting next to me that day was a man wearing a wet wool cardigan. Truthfully, it really only smelled of one thing – his breakfast. Which had been boiled eggs. And if there's one thing guaranteed to make me spew my guts, apart from going to the dentist, it's the smell of boiled eggs. Yet as luck would have it, the man got off after three stops, which was just as well, because I'd been holding my breath for the previous two.

37. The Work Place

Random Thoughts And Themes – shrews. Shrews have such a need for constant energy that should they stop feeding for more than three hours they are at risk of dying from starvation.

As this was the first day of the new year, the campus at Surrey was heaving. I registered my qualies at freshers' registration, which took about fifteen minutes. Then I had a quick gander around the university bookshop, moved on to the college grocery, where I bought two apples and ended up in the refectory.

Now carrying something in one hand is always a pain when you are on crutches. It's such a stupidly frustrating situation, but there's no way you can carry anything safely like a cup of tea. So I was making for the nearest table and just about to pitch my cup into my groin, when a soft treble descanted gently in my ear –

'Would you like to put your cup on my tray?'

I turned and looked into the face of a Giotto seraph.

'Thanks,' I mumbled and felt my face burn.

'Are you a fresher?'

'Yes … You?'

She nodded.

'What are you studying?'

'Speech therapy.'

'I've heard those speech therapy courses are hard.'

'I've heard that too.'

She laughed then, a laugh that had bright eyes and red cheeks. Her name was Amber. A deeply hippy name, that, but I wasn't going to hold having sixties' wild children as parents against her, no, not me. We chatted for a good thirty minutes about our courses and at noon went down into the Austin Pearce Hall and had a chinwag with the Vice-Chancellor, us and about eight hundred others. This on the part of the VC was a memorable effort, in that it was only about three minutes long. Excellent man, I thought. Afterwards Amber and I went down to a little pub close by called The Three Pigeons and there I told her about myself – my tower block – my animals – my life! And she loved it! In fact she wanted to visit Witley Tower that very evening! But we eventually agreed she'd visit me the following weekend after my visit to Plymouth.

'Going to see a friend?' she asked.

'Yes ...' I said, my cheeks suddenly pretending to be a pair of red peppers.

After lunch I met my tutor, Dr Glasscock.

We sat knees almost touching in his cupboard of an office, surrounded by books on every side. There were even books stacked on the floor. He apologised for the cramped conditions and as if on cue a stack collapsed behind him. We laughed. Doc Glasscock was in his early fifties and reminded me of Dr Guttman from The Heath. However, what was different about Glasscock was that he was instantly likeable in a way that Guttman was not. Another reason I took a shine to him was that name. What a trailer! What a tender-truck! No-one else has that label, I know, because it was invented just for him. I could even believe that his mother and father were called Doodleburger or something, anything but Glasscock. Another thing I found comforting about the Doc was that he was very unkempt. For as we talked, I watched a smidgen of salad cream in his hair attempt to join forces with a blob of pickle sitting in his beard. Call me a softy if you like, but his friendly manner, odd surname and unkemptness endeared him to me. Though the good doctor also seemed to be quite an interesting scientist, as he was deeply into evolutionary genetics. So I explained some of my Happy Room research to him and he was fascinated. Of course, I didn't tell him the full extent of the programme, or about my preliminary findings. I would have to get to know him a lot more before I did that, if I ever did that. Yet, generally speaking, he was very enthusiastic and encouraging about my work, which was, of course, one of the reasons for going to university in the first place.

38. Penultimate

Random Thoughts And Themes – population. During the next sixty seconds 98 people will die and 237 will be born. Every minute the planet's population increases by 139.

There was a letter from Kim waiting for me when I got home. She'd also enclosed a Plymouth-London return railway ticket. After I'd had tea, washed, changed and fed the animals, I gave Hillary a ring.

'I think,' said Hillary, 'that Kim is very lonely down there. Who wouldn't be in a strange town?'

'It's not a strange town, she grew up in Plymouth.'

'Yes, but she lived in London for years, so most of the people she knew down there will have grown up and moved away.'

'So because she's feeling out of it, I've got to drop everything and rush down there.'

'Oh, I see, feeling a bit used and abused, are we?'

'A bit, yes …'

'I don't think you're being very considerate. She wants to see you because she's lonely, yes. But she also misses you. The whole thing is probably mixed up with Richard and her trying to do the best for him all the time. It's quite possible that she feels guilty over her brother, she wonders why it isn't her lying there with half her brain paralysed. Anyone would.'

'These invalids, they can blight your life.'

'Does Eva blight yours?'

'It's different with her, I'm all she's got. Richard's got his parents …'

'I didn't know that.'

'Mind you, they're completely useless.'

'So Kim is trapped. She sees that her parents are incapable of looking after Richard and that if it were left to them he'd be shoved in a home, or a hospital somewhere.'

'But why are you telling me this? I know it all already.'

'You just temporarily forgot, that's all.'

On my second day at Surrey, I went down to the student union office to get myself a student card. For the card to be valid, I had to provide a passport-sized photo of myself. I hate that terminally boring process of sitting in those silly little booths. Whenever I use one, I usually end up with photos that either don't look like me or actually don't include me, as at the vital moment I've sneezed or twitched and my head has bounced out of frame. There was one right outside the union office, so, curling with embarrassment, I went inside and sat down on the little stool. And it suddenly struck me that another reason why I don't like photo booths is that they remind me very much of toilet cubicles. Sitting in that confined space is very much like sitting on the toilet and the last thing you want when you're sitting on the toilet is to have your photo taken.

As a matter of fact, this time the snaps were not too bad. I picked the best one, handed it in and got my card, then went to see the college doctor.

The college doctor had asked to see me, which wasn't surprising, considering my medical history. You know, there's one good thing about being a para – you get to see the medical profession up close and are quickly able to spot a duffer, or a talent.

The medical centre was small, yet seemed well equipped, with a gym and a physiotherapy area. There was quite a queue for the doctor's surgery, so I got my name ticked off and then strolled over to the gym. There I watched two girls pump some iron and several blokes successfully row themselves across a carpet.

Twenty minutes later my name was called.

'I've asked to see you, because I wanted to get to know you a little bit,' said Dr Bryant, as he leafed through my encyclopaedic medical file.

'Fine,' I said.

'All things considered, have you any out of the ordinary physical problems?'

'No.'

'How's the travelling to and from Guildford?'

'Fast and comfortable ...'

'So no problems using public transport then?'

'Absolutely not.'

The doctor paused here and read something in my file.

'You don't take any regular medication do you, Dean?'

'No.'

'Not even for your spasticity?'

'It doesn't bother me.'

'Even at night?'

'At night, it usually calms down.'

'Okay, it's nice to meet you and if you've any problems at all, don't hesitate to come and see me, because I'm keen to keep in touch.'

And with that he extended his hand. Now this was a little bit fast and glib for my liking. You don't ask to see someone, keep them waiting nearly half an hour, and then say hello/goodbye all in a few seconds flat. If as a doctor you're that busy, then you're disorganised and a duffer. So right then and there I thought I might test the tensile of this Dr Bryant a little.

'Why?' I said.

'Sorry?'

'Why do you want to keep in touch?'

'Because you're more likely to need my help than other students.'

'How so?'

'Because you're disabled.'

'So because I'm disabled you think I'm less capable of looking after myself than someone able-bodied?'

'No, of course not. But you are more likely to renew a prescription than others.'

'But I've already told you I don't take any prescribed drugs.'

'Not now you don't, but that could change at any time.'

'Unlikely. I have a serious aversion to such things.'

'Well, you also may want to take advantage of the centre for your physiotherapy; in fact I'd like to encourage you to do so.'

'That's the first time you've mentioned that, doctor. Thank you, but it's Unlikely Part Two, as my phizz regimen has a very detailed home-based schedule.'

'You seem well organised, but if for whatever reason you'd like to make use of the centre, please do.'

I let it go. Perhaps he was busy. Why should I care anyway? No reason. Next – the best part of the day – lunch with Amber.

Once again we met in The Three Pigeons and everything about her was black that day. Black shawl, black frock, black plimsolls. The exceptions were her fluorescent-blue fingernails and huge silver earrings which jangled noisily in her ears.

That day I discovered that Amber was an excellent pool player, as she thrashed me three games in a row. Then we sat and gazed out the window at some authentic Guildford traffic and Amber told me about a Special Needs school she'd visited that morning.

'Apparently, we're going to do quite a lot of practical work there,' she said, 'so our tutor thought it best if we popped in and said hello ...'

'How big is the school?'

'Two classrooms, twelve pupils and six teachers.'

'Two to one, eh?'

'Yes, but one to one would be better for some of those children ...'

Then Amber gave me an odd look.

'But I would know all about that?' I said. 'As a matter of fact, I don't, because I've only recently become a para, but lots of my friends have been through the Special Needs mill, so yes, I do know something about it.'

Amber looked embarrassed then and was quiet for a while. So to cheer her up, I told her a funny story about one of my spitting vipers.

That afternoon I had my first lecture. This was the beginning of the science foundation course. But as I read through the schedule I was a little disappointed, for there was nothing there that I hadn't already covered. Though I perked up when the lecturer arrived, for it was the man himself – Doc Glasscock. And as the class settled down and he began on the early scientists and inventors – Davy, Stevenson, Fox Talbot – I noticed a tiny splodge of mashed potato dangling from his tie, trying to attract the attention of a spec of egg mayonnaise on his cuff and was happy.

After the lecture, I stayed behind in the union bar and played a video game or two. They had one particularly interesting machine called BLAZE. The idea was to get several fire-fighters into a burning building to evacuate the occupants without suffering any casualties. The graphics and sound effects were first class, particularly when someone caught fire. In fact I got so engrossed in BLAZE that I stayed later than I intended and when I eventually caught the bus home it was dark. It had also turned misty. And it was real mist too, not smoke or smog, real clouds fed up with the cold sky coming down to hug the warm ground. But just as I turned into our driveway, I saw The Cape again. This time he was suspended from the tenth floor of the building! I just gawped, not believing my eyes. Whoever this man was, he was an athlete, that was for certain. And as I watched, he abseiled down to a window on the fifth floor, pulled it open and disappeared inside.

'THAT'S MY FLAT!' I yelled, collecting my wits with the force of a rabbit chop to the neck.

I hobbled to the lift as fast as I could, which as luck would have it was just arriving, carrying Lenny.

'Hey, what's up!' he yelled, as I threw myself inside.

'Can't stop, Lenny – someone's just broken into my flat!'

I had no idea what I was going to do when I got upstairs, but if he was harming any of my animals, somehow I would harm him.

On the fifth floor landing, shaking so much I could hardly hold my keys, I unlocked the front door. Inside, the flat was dark and completely silent. Which was not a good sign, as there was nearly always some sort of animal noise coming from somewhere. Quickly, I turned on all the lights and searched the place thoroughly. But I found nothing. The Cape was nowhere. Everything was as I'd left it that morning. I checked the kitchen window. Then I heard a movement and spun around, but it was only Ken, stretching himself on top of the fridge.

'Where has he gone, Ken? Is this how he gets inside the building – through our kitchen window?'

I always left the kitchen window open, so it was neat and tidy access and I had a feeling that The Cape had been using it for some time. Without wasting a second, I got out my tool box and nailed the window shut.

39. The Poetry of Flood

Random Thoughts And Themes – the colour red. In England, during the fifteenth and sixteenth centuries, the colour red was felt to have healing powers. The sick were dressed in red clothes and surrounded by as many red-coloured things as possible. Funny, but I always feel good when I wear my red boxer shorts. Honest.

The rehab centre sported a café which was open most days and was quite popular. Every month or so this café produced a theme meal and often as not these were well done. Everyone would dress up, Chinese and Indian meals were a favourite and the Roman feast and Tudor and Elizabethan banquets had been crowded. So when the 'Tex Mex' evening was announced, I put my name down for a ticket straight away.

These special meals were always held in the drop-in, because there tables and chairs were plentiful, so virtually any amount of latecomers could get a seat. Also the toilets and the back door were close, just in case anyone felt like leaving or having a crap in a hurry, which amongst centre users was a useful facility to have. But what a night the Tex Mex evening was! There were old El Paso maps hanging from the walls, ponchos draped behind the doors, even the menus were made of burnt pieces of wood. When I arrived, Ishmael, Lucy and Four-wheel-drive were already settled with Lenny and his sister Josephine, who was dressed in a magnificent flamenco dress with her hair painstakingly braided in tiny bows. We were all in costume, including me (although I was dressed as a beggar, which hadn't taken much doing) and everyone seemed determined to enjoy themselves. Straight away I got stuck into the mescal.

Mescal is the clear spirit that contains a dead agave worm at the bottom of the bottle. The worm looks rather like a fat, elongated fly maggot and is supposed to flavour the drink. Mescal takes a bit of getting used to because it's hot, potent stuff, but after about three glasses I was getting nicely giggly. Then it started. Inevitably we began to discuss Mexico and things Mexican. Four-wheel-drive said he had a rattlesnake skin at home that had come from Mexico, but Lenny challenged this.

'Rattlesnakes come from The United States, not Mexico,' he said.

'But suppose a few wriggled across the border?' said Ishmael.

'Then they would be Mexican rattlesnakes,' confirmed Josephine.

'No,' said Lenny.

'What do you mean, no?' said Four-wheel-drive. 'It's possible, just possible.'

'No it's not. Mexico is far too hot for rattlesnakes,' said Lenny authoritatively. 'They like a warm, even, dry climate. Temperatures in Mexico are far hotter on average than anywhere in North, Central or South America. Consequently, Mexico does not have any rattlesnakes.'

Here we were spared by the food arriving. I had something called Ensenada Skillet, which consisted of spiced sausages, onion-pepper sauce and loads and loads of tiny pancakes. Four-wheel-drive had Nachos – a great mound of ladies' fingers and yellow peppers splashed with a thick yellow sauce. And Lucy had Burritto – chicken covered in a red sauce, topped with what looked like sour cream. Everyone seemed to have something different. I perked up, I was really beginning to get into the swing of things, but unfortunately, the tetchy dialogue with Lenny continued. I don't know how we got around to it, but suddenly he and Josephine were hotly arguing where Mexico was exactly.

'It's in Central America,' said Josephine.

'No, it's in North America,' said Lenny.

'How can Mexico be in North America?' said Four-wheel- drive.

'Because it's part of the North American continental plate, so it's part of the North American continent.'

Here I attempted to rescue things by changing the subject.

'Frida Kahlo, I love her paintings,' I said, shoving a particularly large sausage into my mouth, 'a woman full of all kinds of passions.'

'Wasn't she involved in some sort of horrific road crash?' said Lucy, sucking on a glazed orange pepper.

'That's right,' I said, 'she was travelling on a bus when it was hit by a car. She spent a good deal of her life in a wheel-chair because of it.'

'She was a terrible painter,' said Lenny, tomato sauce pouring down his neck, as if someone had just cut his throat.

'On the contrary,' said Josephine, 'she was a fucking good painter!'

'No,' said Lenny.

'YES!' said Josephine.

'NO!!'

And then the food throwing began. All so deeply unnecessary, of course, but what can you say? Lenny started it and it was quickly taken up by the rest of the room. Consequently, the crockery came after the food, followed by the cutlery, at which stage, for safety's sake, Ishmael, Four-wheel- drive, Lucy and I got under the table.

'You know,' said Ishmael, who was dressed in a purple frock coat and wing-collared shirt, now splattered with food and drink, 'I was hoping for a quiet night.'

'What a sad tosser you are,' said Four-wheel-drive, who was dressed as a set of carracas, down the front of which a portion of chilli sauce was now sliding. 'Don't you realise that it's always going to be like this?'

And it was at that point amid the screaming and mayhem that I noticed two agave worms lying on the carpet. I stared at them hard, for they appeared to be moving.

40. If It Moves, Lobby It

Random Thoughts And Themes – double standards. Let a woman go into a chemists and ask for a packet of tampons and they'll ask her, 'What size do you want – small, regular, super?' But let a man go into the same chemist's and ask for a packet of condoms and do you think they'll ask him what size he wants – small, regular or super? No. Double standard!

It's well known that one way of keeping an issue current is to constantly thrust it into the public eye. Our problem on The Alton was that we'd simply run out of thrustable ideas.

At first, things had gone well. Large articles had appeared in the local papers that debated the Alton Estate Affair in ample detail. There had also been the odd mention in some of the national tabloids plus some coverage on radio and local TV. So the question of what should happen to the estate had not been ignored by the media. The main problem was simply keeping the pot boiling. There were always other stories, other causes. So when Hillary came up with the idea of lobbying our MP, we wondered why we hadn't thought of it before.

Mind you, we all knew that David Parr, MP for Putney and District, wasn't really interested in the fate of the Alton Estate, because we'd exchanged letters with him on several occasions. But Hillary thought it might get a mention here and there if we actually went to the Commons and kicked up some sort of fuss, maybe walked up and down with a placard or two, or had Parr dragged out of a committee meeting to talk to us. It was worth a try and what was more, sounded like a good day out.

We met outside The Montague Arms on the Friday, which I remember was quite a cold morning. Unusually, I was the first to arrive, but as I watched three swans swerve around the church steeple and head out across the common, Lenny appeared.

To get to the House of Commons we borrowed the rehab centre's minibus. There was some argument over who would drive, as no-one wanted to, but in the end it was agreed Hillary would drive there, Lenny would drive back and Eileen and I would share the navigating. So we set off, but just as we were pulling around the church, we saw an old friend – Maddox, Putney Council's Chief Planning Officer. He was walking down Medfield Street holding a clipboard under one arm. Spontaneously, we all hung out of the van's windows and gave him the V-sign. Silly? Yes, but as I've said before, a bit of silliness now and then is good for the psyche. It certainly set us up for the day.

'Fancy a date?' said Lenny, turning to me.

He proffered a paper bag full of what looked like deer droppings.

'Got any oryx shit?' I said.

Lenny smiled. 'That's for lunch.'

We sang songs all the way to Westminster. Songs that were in bad taste and plain daft, but it was then that I discovered that I had quite a reasonable singing voice. It surprised Hillary too –

'You're tone deaf, do you know that?'

'Rubbish!' I said. 'Malicious, heinous, rubbish!'

It took us about two hours to get to the Houses of Parliament, as the traffic was quite thick. When we did arrive it was not a moment too soon, because I was just about to throw up over Eileen, as I suffer quite badly from car sickness. But straight away there was more trouble, as security at the main gate wouldn't let us park inside the palace grounds. We stood up for ourselves, though, and after a furious debate were eventually given permission to park in the Star Chamber Courtyard. This was a pretty little niche with a cobbled floor and basalt archway. From there we made our way through to the Central Lobby, where we had further problems as Lenny had his placard taken away by a policeman. This was a piddling little A4 size job that simply read – 'Save The Alton Estate!'

'It's a polite placard,' Len pleaded.

The policeman agreed, but insisted on keeping it –

'You can have it back when you leave,' he said.

This didn't please Len, but there was nothing to be done.

The situation for lobbying at the House of Commons is quite straightforward – provided the House is sitting, you can turn up at any time and ask to see your MP. No formal arrangements are necessary and provided he/she is there they are obliged to see you. That is the convention. After filling out an MP request form at the Central Lobby, we sat down and suddenly were swept away by the atmosphere of the place. For the Palace really did buzz with action and circumstance, as MPs, researchers and all kinds of ancillary staff hurried back and forth. We even recognised a few faces, who all, funnily enough, wore the same expression, a mixture of intense concentration and self-importance.

'It's busier than I imagined,' said Hillary.

'And there are police everywhere,' said Lenny.

A woman approached us, who looked vaguely like Margaret Thatcher. For a moment, all four of us were mesmerised by the same illusion.

'You've come to see Mr Parr?' asked the Margaret-Thatcher woman.

'That's right,' I murmured.

'I work in his office. I'm afraid he's in an important meeting at the moment and will not be available for some time. Is there any chance that you could come back later?'

'Our problem is that we've come quite a long way,' said Hillary.

'Perhaps you could have lunch and come back?'

'Have lunch where?' said Lenny.

'There are plenty of good restaurants towards Leicester Square.'

'We couldn't afford a restaurant,' said Lenny.

The woman looked hard at Lenny and you could see she was taking in his badly scarred face. Then she stared at me and my crutches. There was no denying it, we were a sad-looking bunch.

'Would you like to have lunch here?' she said, almost apologetically.

'Well, actually we haven't got any money between us,' I said.

I was just wondering how pathetic this must have sounded when the woman smiled.

'Don't worry about that,' she said.

I noticed that the woman had a twitch in one eye, which was gently pulsing down the side of her face, and for a split second I felt sorry for her. But then I remembered that she was the grovelling lackey of David Parr MP and the moment quickly passed.

We were led down a corridor to the Strangers' Restaurant. This was a place of oak panelling, crisp linen tablecloths and good views of the Thames. There we were treated to a fantastic lunch, where Lenny had eaten four bread rolls before the soup arrived and I had a double helping of everything. We also drank five bottles of wine between us as the waiter just kept bringing it. By 1pm we were singing, by 2pm were legless and by 3pm, all sound asleep.

Because of this our lobbying plans were completely banjaxed. And somehow we lost Lenny as he wandered off into the depths of the Palace looking for the gents, so we were forced to leave without him, as the minibus had to be back by a certain time. Though having a final bottle of wine on the road, we did manage to toast him *in absentia*, as it were.

How we got home in one piece, I'll never know. I remember that during this drive a couple of pedestrians did actually bounce off the bonnet, but nobody else will confirm this and the police weren't waiting for us when we got home, so maybe I did imagine it.

Looking back, I think it was all down to Parr and his sly strategy. He kept the rabble off his back by arranging for them to park in the Strangers' Restaurant and eat and drink until they were immobile and therefore harmless. Cunning bastard. Still, we had a laugh or two, which was something.

41. Plymouth Ho!

Random Thoughts And Themes – elm trees. In any given year a large elm tree may exude over 26,000 gallons of moisture. Incredible, eh?

The next morning I caught the tube to Paddington and a train to Plymouth.

As I hadn't been on a real train for some time, I just sat in my seat for the first hour, hypnotised by the streaming scenery. You know there's nothing quite like a long train ride. I also had the entire carriage to myself, which was a good feeling. It was as if the train were travelling just for me, to the extent that when two people got on at Reading, I felt decidedly territorial. Eventually I managed to shake myself awake and did some reading, catching up on the latest *Beautiful Stories for Ugly Children.* There I read about a woman who had mutilated the muscles of her legs and sewn her hands together so she could pray more efficiently. But the closer the train got to Plymouth, the more difficulty I had in concentrating. I pondered this and realised that I was becoming more and more excited at the thought of seeing Kim. This became so acute that by the time the train arrived in Plymouth, I was shaking with anticipation.

She met me on the platform.

'You haven't changed a bit,' I said.

It was true, she looked great.

'Except you've got older,' I added.

'But it's only been three weeks,' she said.

'At your age that's a lot of DNA destruction.'

'Why do I like you?'

Kim's house, on the edge of the city, was just an ordinary

three-bedroomed semi from the outside, but inside had been completely rebuilt. Richard had his own bedroom and activity area, plus a physiotherapy gym with all the latest hoists and exercisers, and in the basement, there was a small heated swimming pool. Money was talking so loudly here that it was giving me earache.

Richard was sitting in the activity area in front of a large video screen. I was taken aback at the sight of him because he really did look amazingly well. At The Heath, he had always looked pasty and lethargic. Here his eyes were bright and he was moving with real co-ordination, as he was actually holding a cup and drinking from it! Furthermore, as I sat on the side of the couch, he laughed at a cartoon on the video screen. He actually laughed! Okay, it was a slightly weird, PVS type of laugh, but it was a laugh and that was a sound I'd never heard him make before. He was making incredible progress and all in three weeks! I was deeply impressed and told Kim so.

In the afternoon the sky looked dark and threatening but we ignored this and took off for a walk along the seafront.

I'd never been to Plymouth beach, so there was a lot to see. Firstly, we burnt off a few calories by racing Richard and his wheelchair along the front. He had two little plastic windmills Sellotaped to each arm of the chair and as they spun fiercely in the wind, we all laughed our heads off. Well, at the time it seemed funny. Then we sat on a bench to get our breaths back and watched seagulls dive-bomb some guillemots. My arms were aching a bit at this stage, as I hadn't had a serious walk on sticks for some time, so I did a few sit-ups right there on the pavement to loosen up.

'How many sit-ups can you do in one go? said Kim.

'About a hundred and forty,' I said.

'Really?'

'Yes, on a good day.'

'You're fit enough to look for crabs then?'

'What, *crab* crabs, the sideways-scuttling things?'

'I bet I can find one before you can.'

'How will we get the wheelchair onto the beach?'

'Oh, Richard can walk now.'

'HE CAN WALK!?!'

'Yes, as long as it's no more than about twenty yards.'

'You never told me.'

'I was saving it.'

This I had to see. And it was true – with sticks and leaning on Kim, Richard actually walked down the stairs to the sand and then over to an old open-air swimming pool, a distance of about 15 yards.

'If only Guttman could see this,' I said, 'he'd choke on his chesterfield.'

Kim laughed and then we were all laughing our heads off again.

Hysterics over, we sat on the edge of the swimming pool, filling our lungs with lung-sized pieces of salty air and listening to the seagulls once more, which were now harassing a dog.

The swimming pool was one of those old Victorian types that use the tide as a filtering system. Long disused, it was now filled with sand and rocks. Good crab territory.

At first we couldn't find anything, though we did come across loads of snakelock anemones with their pretty magenta tentacles. Then I found a small dead fish. Its perfect silver body shone brightly in my hand like a piece of polished metal. I got out my penknife and cut it into three sections.

'Dean, if you're hungry,' said Kim, 'I've got an apple in my bag.'

'Let's see if the anemones are hungry,' I said.

I took a piece of the fish and pushed it towards one of the snakelocks. Quickly the anemone's tentacles bunched around the piece of flesh and worked it towards its mouth. Then suddenly a crab, no larger then a matchbox, appeared from underneath a rock, swiftly straddled the anemone and with great dexterity plucked out the piece of fish with a claw. Kim and I watched amazed.

For a late lunch we went back into town and while Kim found a wall-bank, Richard and I parked in a Spud-U-Like. There we had a cup of tea each and I had a quick decko at a newspaper I found on a table, but suddenly we were being harassed.

'May I sit here?' he said.

I looked up. He was wearing a white Levis jacket, cream trousers and a very wide smile.

'Fine,' I said.

'Thank you so much,' said the man.

He was well mannered, but I found his white clothes offensive somehow.

'Anything interesting going on in the world?' said the man, gesturing at my newspaper.

'No, not really,' I said.

'I never buy newspapers.' he continued. 'I did years ago. I would always buy *The Times*. And years ago it was a good read. But that's all changed now.'

He took a sip of coffee.

'Of course,' he continued, 'the old *Telegraph* was an excellent newspaper, its foreign reporting was unrivalled. In fact, I had a friend who was an assistant reporter on it. This is before the war, of course ...'

'The Second World War, I presume?' I said.

'Oh yes, the Second World War,' said the man, brightening. 'Do you know, he once did a wonderful thing. In 1937 he travelled to Nepal across the Himalayas on a donkey. Nepal was still quite an isolated country then. So I suppose the Nepalese would not have seen a Westerner from one decade to the next. Consequently, for one to suddenly pop up, riding on the back of a donkey, was quite an event.'

'What do you do?' I said, 'if you don't mind me asking?'

'I'm a retired civil servant. I worked for the Entomology department, at the Natural History Museum.'

'Insects?'

'Yes ...'

All at once this man sounded rather interesting.

'They are astounding, you know,' continued the man,

'and could be much more useful than we think. For example, I've always advocated that man would have a much more stable diet if he were to eat insects.'

'*Eat* insects?'

'Well, I've eaten grasshoppers in Algeria. You just pluck off the heads, wings and legs, sprinkle them with pepper and fry them in butter. They are excellent! And I've also eaten the Great Silver Beetle – *Hydrophilus piceus*. And you would never credit it, but the common woodlice have a flavour, when chewed, that is remarkably like shrimp.'

At that moment Kim returned so we had to say goodbye to the insect eater. Absorbing bloke, though, even if he was completely off his head.

We had some tea and a cake in a nearby café and then we went down to the Seaworld Aquarium.

I didn't like this place very much as the fish seemed far too cramped and crowded in their tanks, which is often the case with aquariums. I was particularly pissed off to see a conger eel in a tank so small that it could not stretch out without touching the sides. One of the frequent mistakes that fish keepers make is to assume that fish are stupid. This is a bad error, as they need just as many distractions and amusements as other animals.

After visiting the aquarium we went for a walk along the coast towards Bigbury Bay. The sun came out in some strength at this point, which was pleasant, although after we'd covered a couple of miles, Kim was kind to my arm muscles and suggested we stop for a while. Which we did, letting the sea breeze gently cool our faces.

When we got back to the house I had a swim in the swimming pool, which woke me up. Then Kim and I changed, me into another grubby T-shirt, her into a clean one and leaving Richard with a sitter, we caught a taxi into town.

'I'm going to treat you,' said Kim.

'You've been treating me ever since I've known you.'

'I do spoil you, don't I?'

The taxi pulled up outside a restaurant called Dinner

Money. Inside the place was decorated like a school class-room, with desks for tables and a blackboard on the wall. There was even a 'shop' in one corner with packets of soap powder and jars of jam and Marmite.

Kim had reserved a table, so we were quickly seated and served by a waitress wearing a St Trinian's type uniform.

'What's the food like here?'

'Terrible,' said Kim, smiling at the waitress who instantly smiled back, 'but it's meant to be terrible.'

'That's right,' said the waitress, 'the food's utterly horrible.'

'If the food's so bad,' I said, 'why is everybody smiling so much?'

'The atmosphere,' suggested the waitress.

'Yes, the crack,' said Kim.

I was still a bit baffled, but Kim ordered bacon rissoles, greens and chips, so I went ape-shit and ordered spam fritters, swede and mashed potatoes.

'This will be the first time I've eaten a spam fritter,' I said.

'Stay calm, won't you?' said Kim.

At that moment, there was a commotion at another table. The head waiter, dressed as a schoolmaster, complete with gown and mortarboard, was holding a customer by the ear.

'WHAT'S YOUR NAME?' bellowed the head waiter.

'Rick Taylor,' said the customer, giggling.

'SPEAK UP!'

'RICK TAYLOR!!'

'Taylor, you snivelling little tyke. You'll eat every scrap of your cabbage, do you hear, boy?'

'Yes …'

'YES, WHAT?'

'YES, SIR!'

When the food arrived, I'd been given three domed dollops of mashed potato served from a scoop.

'The portions are quite small,' said Kim. 'I forgot to mention that. Hope it's going to be enough for you?'

'Stop worrying,' I said. 'I'm having a great time. But if I puke my ring, just ignore me.'

'Don't you dare throw up, because if you do, a middle-aged, barrel-thighed nurse will appear and cart you off to the sick room.'

'You know what I can't believe?'

'What?'

'That people are actually paying good money for all of this.'

For dessert Kim had tapioca pudding, while I had Manchester tart with custard.

'I've never had tapioca pudding before,' said Kim, resting her spoon alongside her half-finished bowl. 'I think I know why now.'

'The trouble with the world today,' I said, 'is that no-one has custard with anything any more.'

We got back to the house at about 12.30am. Kim paid the sitter, while I went upstairs to the flat.

I really liked Kim's flat. It was functional without being too neat or minimalist. The sofa was particularly good. It was a saggy flop-all-over-me type. So I did. Could I live in a place like this, I asked myself? I don't see why not, I replied.

When Kim had checked Richard, she came upstairs and opened a bottle of wine.

'I really did miss you, you know,' she said, sitting down beside me.

'Seriously?' I said.

'Of course.'

Kim poured the chilled white wine into two glasses and handed me one. Instantly, through the glass, I felt the cold of the wine begin to numb the palm of my hand. I looked at Kim.

'I've missed you too,' I said.

'You're just copying me.'

'No, I'm not. I would never say anything like that unless I really meant it. When the train was approaching Plymouth, I was shaking.'

'That was worn axles and clapped out suspension.'

'No, it was excitement.'

'Really?'

'Of course.'

Here Kim put her glass down, leaned across the sofa and kissed me on the lips. This quickly became heavy stuff, with her tongue doing all sorts of things inside my mouth, while at the same time her hands were smoothing down my back and thighs. I took a quick straw-poll on this and found my mouth, back and thighs were all in favour.

'Will you sleep with me?' said Kim.

'Certainly.'

'Really?'

'Really. But guess what? I've never slept with anyone before.'

'You've got to do it sometime, you know.'

'I've been saying that for ages. This is the first time anyone's listened.'

Kim laughed, but suddenly those old-fashioned brass bells were ting-a-linging in my head again and I began to feel warm. Too warm.

'You haven't forgotten that I'm a para, have you, Kim?'

Kim stared into my face wide-eyed. 'I don't think so.'

Then I went straight for it, with just a single snatch of oxygen for balance.

'We've never discussed this,' I said, 'but I have damage in my spinal cord which relates to all the nerves in my thighs. I can't get an erection, Kim, and I'll never be able to.'

With all the information that she must have collected looking after Richard, I was sure she would have come across it – that a high percentage of paraplegic males with spinal injuries are impotent. Yet as I looked into her face, I knew she hadn't. It was a pisser on an enormous, urino-genital scale. And there's no real way around it. You see, coition was invented with mammals in mind, in the sense that they're psychologically designed for the intense emotional highs and lows. Other animals just nob and run. Not so mammals, because they develop – via sexuality –

much deeper relationships, so when coition is removed from a mammal's life, its emotional health is in jeopardy. And legends that those that can't perform full sex can do 'other things' are a crass load of wet bog roll. There are certain mammalian physiological processes that have no substitute. Shagging is one of them.

At about 3am, I was still awake, my mind simply refused to relax in any way. I just lay there on the bed in the spare room, blinking into the dark. Every now and then little things would come back to me. College. Eva. Kim. Mostly Kim. I tried hard to stop them, but the auto-thoughts were too strong. Then I began to sweat. Then swim in my sweat. Swim in the warm pool of the bed, heart racing, lungs pulling for breath. The undersheet became rucked up and uncomfortable, so I turned on my side and sat up. I got to my feet and hopped across to the window and pulled it open. The cold air and noise of the night roared into the room fast and loud. I had some sleeping pills in my bag, so I emptied them out across the dressing table. I picked one up and rolled its shiny body between my fingers. It was pert and fat like a lava. I stretched a hand along the top of the dresser, smeared the wood grain with my moisture and then with a sip of wine, swallowed all of the capsules, one after another.

I went back to the bed and lay down again. Within a few minutes, a dense foam began to seep into me. I began to lap and surge with it and then calmly let go as an opaque film sheathed my consciousness and my whole body began to slip smoothly into a fast pouring darkness.

I left Plymouth on the Sunday at midday. Kim saw me off at the station. She said things to me and I said things to her, none of which I'm going to repeat here. It's enough to say that if I ever needed an erase button for my life it was then. Oh, and by the way, don't ever try and top yourself with sleeping pills that you've been heavily abusing for years. All that happens is that you wake up in the morning feeling like a pool of bird vomit.

42. The Beginning of the Ending

Random Thoughts And Themes – the colour of death. Some animals, when dying, change colour. The mullet is known for this. In fact the Roman Emperor Thespasian once had a live mullet brought to his table in a vase of water and then amused his dinner guests by having the water slowly removed, causing the fish to become a kaleidoscope of colour. Nice man, eh?

I got back to Roehampton on the Sunday evening to again discover police cars slewed across Witley's driveway. As I approached the front doors a PC opened them from the inside.

'Dean McAdam?'

I nodded.

'Do you know Mr Leonard Underwood?'

'I do, what's happened?'

'When did you see him last?'

Lenny had gone missing – no-one had seen him for three days. The policeman asked me where I'd been for the weekend. I told him about the Plymouth trip and had to give him Kim's address and phone number. He also asked me about the visit to the House of Commons. I knew what he was thinking, but told him that although Lenny hadn't come back with us, he'd made it home that evening, because I'd spoken to him on the phone.

Two disappearances from the block in little more than two weeks! Webley, I had no real thoughts on, or frankly much motivation to worry over, but Lenny was different; he was my friend. There was a chance, just a chance, that he was holed up with one of his old Fulham mates. He'd attended a Mind centre there at one time and still kept in touch with some of its users. I told the policeman this and prayed that was what had happened.

In the flat everyone seemed pleased to see me. Even Ken. From the top of the fridge he cocked his head to one side, as if to say, 'Hello, nice to see you.' Then Rachel sloped by. I couldn't put my finger on it, but somehow she looked different. It was to do with the way she was moving. Sluggish. I picked the gecko up. There was a slight swelling of the stomach and engorgement of the neck. No, it couldn't be! She was pregnant! Though how she'd got in with the other geckos, was something I didn't understand. But I was pleased. Reptiles will often not breed in captivity, so any chance of a birth was exciting. And this would be Rachel's first.

I went through to The Happy Room. While I'd been away I'd let a control experiment run in the insect arena.

Wasps and spiders were good material for my programme as their physiologies and behaviour patterns have many parallels. They are also deadly enemies, which was another good reason for using them.

If left alone in controlled conditions wasps and spiders will attack each other and fight to the death. One interesting point about these battles is that provided the insects are basically the same size, the battle is fairly even. For instance, if the wasp manages to mount the spider's back, then it will be all over in seconds as the wasp will quickly behead the spider with his jaws. But if the wasp attacks the spider from virtually any other angle, then he is in great danger, for the spider will swivel, seize him with his mandibles and inject him with paralysing venom, etc. So bearing this in mind, using a magnifier mounted on a clamp, I spiked the mandibles of three orb spiders and the stings and jaws of three hunting wasps with blobs of superglue. Then I put them in the insect arena.

At first, as normal, the insects repeatedly attacked each other, but through lack of effective weaponry, soon got bored. Finally, the wasps sucked some sugar and the spiders drank from a saucer of milk, and when I returned they were all bunched together in the soft earth of the arena, sleeping soundly.

Now more and more, I was convinced that there wasn't a behavioural cycle in the entire animal world that couldn't be influenced by a bit of lateral biology!

I cleared up the arena, put the insects away and began writing the experiment up in the Happy Room Lab Log. I hadn't got further than a few sentences when suddenly a Roman candle burst outside the window in a huge flower of flames. I hobbled across to the window. Beyond the grass square, a team of about fifteen Ashburton Boys crescented the driveway. They were back! But as I gazed down at them they were closing on two figures – Four-wheel-drive and Ishmael.

43. The Battle of Witley Tower

Random Thoughts And Themes – things that I love. My sister. My animals. Sunshine. Laughing. Holidays. Routemaster buses.

When I got downstairs the air was full of smoke and shouts as the ABs hurled a whole range of fireworks, half-bricks and chunks of paving stones at Ishmael and Four-wheel-drive, who deftly attempted to field them with baseball bats.

Degs and Two Para were there. And so were some others from the Blackford's Path crew, their raw red scars making them look hard and nasty. As I opened the ground-floor door a large jagged stone struck Ishmael on the shoulder and hissed past my ear. The ABs cheered. But at that moment a boy was smashed across the head by a canvas bag that seemed to plunge out of the sky. He collapsed as the bag split open and sprayed a nauseous yellow liquid everywhere. Swiftly Degs pulled out a handgun from his jacket, swung it upwards and fired. There was a pause, followed by the sound of something crashing down the side of Witley. It was The Cape! Degs had shot The Cape! The ABs yahooed, assuming the flasher was one of us. However, spread-eagled on the pavement, bloody, quite dead and with his mask ripped from his face, was Mr Maddox, Putney Council's Chief Planning Officer. Then all at once Degs was hit by another flying canvas bag and he too collapsed. Again, nauseous liquid showered everywhere. I looked up at the block. Far in the distance of the upper floors I glimpsed a familiar head. Then police sirens began to wail and everyone bomb-burst.

Ishmael, Four-wheel-drive and I scrambled towards the block. I swiped the door with my card-key and we fell inside. Four-wheel-drive and I tried to stem the blood as it pumped thickly from Ishmael's shoulder, while all laughing maniacally.

'Why're you laughing?' I said, to Ishmael.

'Because you are.'

'I'm laughing because it's funny.'

'What's funny?' said Four-wheel-drive.

But we all burst out laughing again.

Vile met us at the sixth floor. He was bouncing up and down like a beach ball.

'Did you see Degs go down?' he said, gleefully.

'Yeah,' I said, 'and I have a feeling he may not be getting up again.'

'Sounds sweet to me …' murmured Ishmael.

Once inside Vile's flat we had a closer look at Ishmael's shoulder. The skin was quite badly gashed, but there didn't seem to be any fractures. I did the field nurse bit and tore up one of Vile's sheets for a bandage. I'd always wanted to do that. But when I'd finished, Ishmael looked more uncomfortable than when I'd started, though admittedly it did stem the bleeding.

'By the way, what was the liquid in the canvas bags?' I said.

'Yeah, it smelled really fucking bad,' said Four-wheel.

'I hope it wasn't corrosive or anything,' I added, 'because I got it all over me.'

'Dog piss,' said Vile, matter-of-factly.

After we'd made Ishmael reasonably comfortable on the sofa, Vile broke out some of his home-made brandy. I protested at this, as I knew just how poisonous Vile's distillations could be, but I was howled down. The problem with Vile's home-made spirits was that you had to pace yourself really carefully, or you'd soon become hopelessly drunk after just a few glasses. Unfortunately, we didn't get around to discussing this, so within twenty minutes Four-wheel-drive and Ishmael were comatose.

'You shouldn't give people this stuff without a written warning, Vile,' I complained, as I put a cushion under Ishmael's head.

'They've only had two glassfuls each,' said Vile, plainly disgusted.

He went to a cupboard and took out two cut glasses and a bottle of Laphroaig.

'I've been saving the bio-stuff for a decent celebration,' he said. 'This could be it.'

I looked closely at the bottle.

'Is this real Laphroaig?'

'As close as you can make this side of the border. Walk this way …'

Vile began to stroll down the hallway.

'Where are we going? And shouldn't we keep an eye on things? I mean things have become really serious.'

'If you haven't noticed, things have been really serious here for a long time. Anyway, with the card-key system down and the stairs out to the first floor, the building is just about impregnable.'

'I didn't know the card-key system was down.'

'Yeah, I pulled my tongue through the dispenser five minutes ago.'

44. Battle Floor

Random Thoughts And Themes – sleeping. Have you ever thought how sleeping is the most perfect state to be in? You're not eating, drinking or going anywhere, so there's little cost involved. Furthermore, you can dream any situation or any place without the hassle or stress of actually going there. There should be sleep clubs, sleep cafés, sleep shops (just another thought).

At basement level 1, we got out of the lift and made our way to the spiral stairway. I looked down into the blackness and once again there was that familiar smell of dust and piss.

'The hash field?' I said.

'Same floor, different part,' said Vile.

'There's more space beyond the field?'

'These basements go on forever.'

Once more we climbed down the spiral stairs.

'Do you know,' said Vile, 'everything is numbers.'

'What?'

'There's maths in everything.'

I paused for a moment to get my breath. The key to going down a spiral stairway on crutches is to do a sort of downward hop. This consists of launching the crutches and your body consistently downward. So for every step you take, you have the sensation of actually diving into blackness, which takes a bit of doing.

'And mortality,' continued Vile, 'is directly dependent on impulses that are so mathematical, that were it possible to conceive the mechanism, you could predict its extent to the last second.'

For a moment, I gripped the handrail tightly and imagined straddling it, then corkscrewing into the dark. The problem would be controlling the speed, for it was such a tight spiral that you'd soon be travelling so fast you'd almost certainly damage yourself at the end. Or perhaps swerve off halfway and free-fall.

'For example, how many times have you blown your nose?'

'Vile, what are you babbling on about?'

'Do you know how many times you've blown your nose?'

'Don't be a prat.'

'But there will be a number. From the time your mother first blew your nose for you, to whatever age you are now, you'll have blown your nose a certain number of times.'

'So what? It means nothing.'

'Not quite. Everyone's life is an equation that equals a certain number of tasks and performances.'

'So a man scratches his left ear 1,536 times and touches daffodils sixty-one times in his life – that means something? Puerile psychobabble. Knowledge without imagination is worthless.'

Vile grinned. 'I can imagine all kinds of knowledge.'

At Basement level 3, we passed the Roe. The slender, fast-moving river glittered darkly and for a moment I wondered how it could move so swiftly without making even the faintest sound. Then I began to smell it. That amazing, sickly fragrance of five thousand opium poppies.

At level 4, when the lights were switched on, the plants seemed even taller than I remembered.

'That's because they've grown since you last saw them,' said Vile. 'They'll stop growing at about five and three quarter feet.'

As we crossed the field I thought I was seeing things. It's amazing how your senses can play tricks on you, but every now and then I could have sworn I caught a movement out of the corner of my eye, like the glint of an insect, or the flash of a bird's wing. Yet whenever I turned, there was nothing.

Vile led me to another large room beyond the poppy field. There, almost the entire floor space – 100ft square – consisted of a huge polythene tank filled with water.

'What's all this?' I said, thumping my hand against the side of the tank.

Facing each other at one end of the tank stood a pair of flush-mounted consoles. These sported aerials nearly 10ft high and floating inside the tank, side by side, lay two 4ft long model submarines.

'The models …' drawled Vile, 'are controlled via eight-channel transmitters and driven by triple electric motors. They go forward, reverse, turn 360 degrees, do the same underwater and have a top speed of about scale forty knots. And watch the control, because it really is fingertip. Now they carry a single impact torpedo, which will move at scale seventy knots and contains $\frac{1}{8}$ ounce of semtex.'

'$\frac{1}{8}$ ounce of semtex?' I said.

'$\frac{1}{8}$ ounce of sem is enough to blow these models into matchwood,' Vile continued. 'If they were made of matchwood, that is. But they're not, they're made of perspex, which will shatter like glass. So be careful.'

I was touched. Vile was being considerate. It was his first time.

I soon found out why the subs were made of perspex. For there was a reason, no matter how warped, for everything Vile did – each model contained a small flooded compartment and swimming inside this was a baby red piranha fish. 'You have to do it, don't you?'

Vile chuckled. 'Just my little joke.'

Again there were detailed score cards giving points for damage. I liked the idea of one torpedo. It was more final. More do or die. There would be much less messing about with this game.

'Right,' I said, 'the same two questions. How long do I get to practise? And what's the combat duration? Oh, and do I get a dummy shot?'

'Five minutes. Ten minutes. No.'

Vile was right – the piranha subs were fast and highly

manoeuvrable. Mine would dive in two seconds, resurface in the same time and move across the water like a hydrofoil. The models were much slower underwater, of course, but still surprisingly swift.

True to his word, after five minutes, Vile blew a klaxon and we were off. He'd demanded a start with the boats equidistant, moving along the surface of the water. Then after three turns of the pool, we simultaneously dived both models.

There we paused, the subs drifting just below the surface like pike, sly for prey. It was then that I realised that underwater, because of the clear perspex structure, the boats possessed a certain refractive quality, which made manoeuvring difficult, because you were never quite sure whether what you were seeing was exactly what was going on. This was good in a way, because it added another element to everything.

Slowly, at quarter power, Vile's model edged towards mine. So I advanced at quarter power towards his. We were 30ft apart. Twenty. Fifteen. At ten, I knew that if he fired his torpedo, even at that range, with one flick of my thumb, I could veer my sub out of danger. But suddenly, at full power, his boat leapt at mine, yet at barely 6ft apart, I dived and Vile's model raced harmlessly above. I quickly turned and resurfaced just as Vile's sub dived. Instantly, I sped my boat across the pool and hovered directly over his. Then I blew my forward tank and my model's bows – holding the lethal torpedo – dipped towards his. But Vile guessed my plan and dodged his sub away in reverse. Not letting him off the hook, I followed. Then I dived again and came down on top of his conning tower, giving it a good crack with my bows. Once more Vile reversed his model away, resurfaced at the other end of the pool and then swung around in a long curve. I resurfaced too and turned to face the enemy.

Vile and I grinned at each other from our consoles. Finally, our subs were 15ft apart. Ten. Seven. At 5ft we pressed our release switches, there was a bang, the miniature torpedos leapt into the water but at virtually zero range, we swerved our models sideways and the deadly missiles ploughed past their targets, streaked to opposite ends of the tank and impacted against its polythene walls. Vile hadn't anticipated this. The two explosions were muffled, but the effects were devastating – the 100ft long tank immediately split in two and Vile and I were suddenly engulfed in 4000 gallons of water.

For a few moments, we were struggling, as the water avalanched all around us. Then it found two drains in a corner and as I grasped a doorframe and Vile clung to some dexion shelving, the water began to whirlpool violently into the floor.

'How do you score that one!?!' I shouted, above the roar.

'Very, very carefully!' yelled Vile, his wet hair streaking his face like rats' tails.

It took a full ten minutes before the water was low enough for us to get out of the room. Then Vile opened the door to the opium field and we paddled out. I was utterly soaked, and colder and stiffer than a cadaver from Christianshab (that's a small town in western Greenland). But Vile began to laugh.

'Is it funny?' I said.

'Yes.'

'You want to die, don't you?'

'Why should I want to die?'

'Because deep down, you're a death-and-glory freak. It's obvious. You're a closet hero, Vile, and the evidence is quite damning. Your preferred film genres are War and Westerns. Your all-time favourite celebs are Tin Tin and John Noakes. And you've always worn your sandals without socks.'

'Still do,' said Vile, wagging a sockless foot.

Then Vile offered me his latest hallucinogen, and for a moment a leopard-coloured capsule growled softly in the palm of my hand.

'No thanks, Vile,' I said, handing the capsule back. 'Colour scheme's nice, though.'

Vile shook his head in mock disdain, swallowed the capsule and then I watched him slowly and gently lower himself to the floor. At that moment I felt dizzy, so I went over to the Venus-flytrap urinal and put my head underneath a tap. Slender fingers of freezing cold clasped my skull like an icy hand.

As the dizziness began to ebb, I stared out onto the poppy field. Just to be able to stand and look at it was far-fetched. How just one man was responsible was the improbable part. Yet Vile was strictly improbable whichever way you looked at him. It was then that the blast door caught my eye.

It was on the other side of the field set in a recess. I hopped across to the huge steel slab. Unless my eyes were playing up again, it appeared to be slightly ajar. I ran my fingers along the rim – yes, it was open. I put my shoulder to it and, with a series of squeals, the massive door yawned wide. What stretched before me then was a cross between a darkened passageway and a cave. I got my pen-torch out, stuck it between my teeth and slowly inched inside.

The floor of the passageway was dirt, there was a strong smell of rotting vegetation and a humming sound like a generator spinning coming from somewhere. After about 40ft the passageway ended in a door. I pushed at this, fumbled for a light switch and found myself standing inside a sound studio. There were mikes on booms, wall-mounted speakers and at the far end a tiny control room. I picked my way across the cable-strewn floor to this and pulled the door open. Everything was lit up and humming – consoles, CD decks, nagras, 1 inch reel to reel. I switched one of the nagra decks on – techno boomed out from quad speakers. I passed on to another deck. This was full of snatches of radio and TV news – bomb blasts, missing yachts, missing children. I went from machine to machine – more techno, some TV sitcom stuff and suddenly I was listening to Webley. Yes, the missing caretaker. It was as if he was being interviewed, but he was talking as if out of breath, as if he'd been running up the stairs and suddenly a mike had been shoved in his face I spun on. All at once Webley was screaming, screaming with pain. I punched the stop button. The deck clicked to a halt and a second or two later the big 1 inch reel to reel stopped too. I turned. I hadn't noticed, but the 1 inch was locked up to the nagras. Someone had been mixing onto it. I pressed the play button of the bulky reel to reel and then I heard Webley screaming with snatches of techno, news interviews, even the Blue Peter theme. Then he was pleading, begging. It was horrible.

'You've found it then,' said Vile, coming up behind me.

I punched the STOP button of the big 1 inch.

'Fuck off!' I shouted, spinning round. 'You've led me here. What have you done with Webley?'

'The sound of suffering, it's extraordinary, isn't it?'

'What did you do to him?'

'Dean, you're the only one that can understand this. It's a bit off the wall, I know.'

'You killed Lenny too, didn't you?'

'No, he topped himself.'

'He topped himself!?!'

'It was his face scarring and his illness. He'd had enough. So he killed himself and we put it on tape.'

'You taped his death?'

'Yeah.'

A pulse like a techno rhythm was now beating in my head.

'How did he die?'

'I injected him with 300mls of heroin straight into the cerebral cortex. He blew like the sun, then lifted off like a comet.'

'Play it to me.'

'Now look …'

'I said – play it to me.'

Vile stretched over to a cassette deck and tapped it on with a finger. There was the sound of a storm blowing, wind squalling and flapping, with slow techno in the background and then a low moaning sound in the foreground which got louder and louder until it was a wild, high-pitched wail of laughter …

I stabbed at the cassette's control panel and it slid to a standstill. The sudden silence echoed loudly in the phone box of the room.

'It was incredible, Dean. Really.'

'And what about Webley?'

'What about him?'

'You killed him. Murder is wrong, Vile. There is no way that it can be justified.'

'But in his case it seemed such a kindness …'

'You're wrong. WRONG!'

I stared hard at Vile until the cadaverous-grey, confident expression on his face began to dissolve. All the drugs-hassle and craziness were coalescing into one huge, irrevocable truth – Vile was off his trolley, bats, barmy, away with the fairies. But then suddenly I found myself not giving a shit. Yes, I know I probably wanted certifying too. But you see, I'd grown up with Vile and he was a cripple long before I was. Furthermore, he was probably right – in Webley's case, topping the bastard might have been a kindness.

'Come on,' I said, 'let's go …'

Fifteen minutes later we were in the lift and as we approached the ground floor I smelled burning. I brought the lift to a halt and peered down the stairs. Beside the ground-floor landing door, threads of black smoke seeped from a section of fractured ducting. Then there was a terrific crack, bricks punched out of the wall and a man's face appeared wearing a hard hat. I glanced out of the landing window – across the square, in the falling evening light, I saw the unmistakable shapes of two swing-ball cranes and dozens of men swarming around them.

Upstairs, Vile and I quickly shook Ishmael and Four-wheel-drive awake. They were both suffering from Vile's vile brandy and it was a shame to move Ish with that shoulder, but it couldn't be helped. So with Claire on a lead, the four of us took the lift down again.

Through the Fish Room windows the dusk sky was cher-ryade, fizzing the tanks red as we began to systematically empty each of them, putting the fish down the outlet that burbled in the middle of the landing. It was a shame to let the baby sea horses go. And I wasn't happy about the trop-ical fish, as they probably wouldn't survive. But what was the alternative? We left Julie until last.

It may seem totally stupid to anyone reading this, but that conger eel was as dear to me as Ken or Rachel. I went across to her tank and put my hand in the water. There was a pause and then the enormous eel slid smoothly under-neath my fingers. I marvelled at the good shape she was in. But she would need to be fit for what was about to happen to her. For with a large net between us, Ishmael and I lifted the great fish out of the tank and carried her across to the outlet pipe.

Surprisingly, she didn't struggle as she disappeared into the blackness of the opening. I imagined her astonishment as she splashed into the Roe and her panicky swim towards the wonderful scent of the sea, which whirled and foamed in the Thames 4 miles away. That would be the first time she had tasted her natural home.

On the third floor, the insects weren't much of a problem, as we bundled all the spiders into a single aquarium, just keeping the Sydney funnel web separate. The mantises and poisonous centipedes had to be packed separately too, but the rest – assorted stick insects, milli-pedes and beetles – I lumped together.

'What now?' said Ishmael.

'Reptiles, second floor.'

A few minutes later as we began clearing the reptiles, Ishmael turned to me, and for a moment a shadow cut across his pale face.

'Are you okay?' I said.

'Yeah, fine.'

I checked his makeshift bandage, but there was no leakage.

'What sort of snake is this?' he said.

He was holding a small tank in one hand which contained a medium-sized snake.

'A puff adder.'

'Is it dangerous?'

'Only if it bites you.'

'Then what?'

'You die in three minutes.'

'I get a whole three minutes?'

'Considerate, isn't it?'

At that moment, a megaphoned voice boomed from downstairs –

'DEAN McADAM AND JOHN DE VILE! THIS IS THE POLICE. I MUST WARN YOU THAT THE BUILDING IS ON FIRE. PLEASE MAKE YOUR WAY TO AN EXIT IMMEDIATELY!!'

'How about that?' said Four-wheel-drive, hopping through the doorway. 'I've always loved a good bonfire.'

We struggled to shake all the reptiles into just five small tanks. The main problem was the baby monitor lizards. They'd rolled themselves into a tight knot and were not budging. In the end we shoved them in with the geckos. There were protests, but it couldn't be helped. Then we shared out the tanks between the four of us and made our way to the Mammal Floor.

'By the way,' said Vile, 'the honey buzzards didn't want to go.'

'That's right,' said Four-wheel, 'they kept flying back in the window.'

'So where are they now?'

'Flying around the building, I think.'

On the Mammal Floor the mice were a problem because there were so many of them, but I eventually squeezed them into two aquaria, which I levered into a rucksack. Then Vile took the rabbits and the chinchillas, Four-wheel took the bush baby, Nose, Ken, and the shrews (which definitely couldn't be put in with anything else) and Ishmael carried the ferrets, tree squirrels and some insects. Lastly, we all piled into the lift.

Curiously, as if we were an extraordinarily heavy load – which we were not – the lift seemed to be moving much more slowly than usual. As if to emphasise this, while passing the eighth floor, the car touched the side of the shaft with a nerve-scraping sound and then, between the tenth and the eleventh floors, rocked to a halt.

'Shit,' said Four-wheel, 'what's up?'

Vile stabbed at the buttons but to no avail, so he prised opened the control panel.

'The scabs,' he said, 'they've cut the juice …'

'Well, we'll have to walk,' I said.

'Walk?' said Ishmael.

'Hop then …'

We pulled the door open and scrambled down onto the tenth floor landing, carefully passing the animals out and stacking them up all around us.

Ishmael and Four-wheel were fitter than I'd realised. They sprang up the steps on a single crutch each. Vile and I had trouble keeping up with them.

'What's the advantage in having a pair of lungs that work at 110%?' protested Vile.

'At Christmas, you get to blow up all the balloons,' said Four-wheel.

'Yeah, and on birthdays,' added Ishmael, 'you can blow out your candles from the next room.'

At first, our footsteps echoed dully amidst the rubbish and broken glass that was scattered everywhere. But the higher we climbed, the more the rubbish receded and was replaced by a thick, soft layer of moss. Here even the windows were covered, not with the moss, but with a slimy algae that made an odd frothing sound when touched.

On the fifteenth floor landing, a suitcase sprawled across the stairs, spewing a vest, underpants and socks like entrails.

'I once had a vest that colour,' said Ishmael.

Four-wheel paused. 'I'm still wearing underpants that colour,' he said.

To get to the twentieth floor, we had to go down on our hands and knees, because from the nineteenth floor up all the steps were completely shattered as if they'd been bombed. But when we finally arrived a surprise was awaiting us because there were rags of skins, cages of bones and knuckles of gristle strewn all over the place. It looked like an abattoir.

'Did a lion live here?' said Four-wheel, kicking a very large collarbone.

'Or a butcher,' I suggested.

'What's that smell?' said Ishmael.

A very fine mist of smoke was climbing through several gaps in the floor. I took a deep breath. It smelled very, very sweet.

'No,' I said, 'it can't be …'

'Yes, it is …' said Vile, grinning.

For a moment, we four stood and inhaled the pure, sweet fumes of 5,000 burning opium poppies. It was the best blow I've ever had in my life.

The roof door swung open with a loud creak, lifting a flock of birds from the elevator heads. They were all there – my kestrels, kites, goshawks, sparrow hawks, peregrine falcons and even the honey buzzards. I counted them as they circled the building and came to rest on the rooftop once more. Then I turned to look at the view. In the closing sunset, all the tower blocks of The Alton were glowing a gentle pink like five enormous chandeliers.

'Look at the bottom of Hilsea and Dunhill,' said Four-wheel.

I stared across at the tower blocks. The blaze at Witley was reflected in their lower windows. Flames 50ft high swam soundlessly like something from a silent film. And then I heard the bells ringing. It was Witley's old fire alarm system activating at last. There were more bells, or rather sirens, as a convoy of emergency vehicles approached the estate from across the common, but at the Roehampton Lane turn-off there was a smash! Some of the emergency vehicles actually crashed into each other! We whistled and hooted. What a cock-up! And all at once a verse came to me. I flicked out my notebook and began to scribble fast –

one morning they came with their silver wheels
and needles and took her to a bright echoey room
there they manhandled her, put things into her
but with coldness, no love

there she dreamt a dream of dreaming backwards
beyond adolescence, beyond infancy
back to a very special room
where she was whole and nothing but whole –
she caught chrome in the delta of dark
from an orbit's core with a moon mad belly …

Ishmael was looking over my shoulder.

'I'll show you a poem,' he said.

And with that, in one go, he pulled his shirt off and we all whistled again, for his entire torso was covered in tattoos, like Rod Steiger in *The Illustrated Man*. But it was a single picture – Hieronymus van Aeken's Paradise, the painting from the Courtauld. The glorious fountain spouted at the tree of Ishmael's neck, the first Man and Woman kneeled in the swells of his chest and gentle creatures grazed peacefully in the valley of his navel. But all at once there were real animals all around us – mice, chinchillas, shrews, tree squirrels, armadillos, lizards, a cat, a gecko and a hedgehog. I stared at these and then belly-flopped out into the darkness.

You know, it's amazing how the air loves you when you fly. You feel its little resistances and pressures all over. From 600ft high, sitting in the night dark, I gazed down at Witley and watched the flames lick the seventh floor clean like a great big animal cleaning a great big bone. I rolled over in the cool evening sky then and looked at the village upside down. Twinkling lights twinkled back and all at once I dived, spine bowing, clothes snapping hard.

The High Street was deserted, except for a black cat sitting on a wall by The Angel. But the lights of the Double Bubble were still glowing, so I drifted across the road.

Inside the café glittered. Ashtrays gleamed on spotless tables, dishcloths fluttered, walls swelled like sails. And at the centre of this magnificent barge, wrapped in pure white linen, stood Maurice. He looked up at me, smiled and then I knew I must travel …

'Doesn't the horizon look amazing,' said Evangeline, shielding her eyes.

'Yes, all those mauve clouds …' said my mother.

'Dean, do you have to walk so fast? Dean!'

From the top of the incline you could see the site clearly, a bracelet of sand stones around a circle of scrubby grass. Here eleven levels of wall striated beneath us. Eleven ancient gardens powdered beneath the dunes. Dotted around the circle of grass, olive and fig trees swayed together and flowers – white clover, pink vetch, wild thyme – sprouted a dazzling patchwork. Just beyond the wall's southern edge a dark-coloured goat was tethered, while three pied goats grazed beside it. There were no apple trees or lotus flowers, but in the middle of the circle stood a single huge pear tree nearly 50ft high.

In the eastern corner of the garden, a cloud of violet butterflies encircled a dry well, which was canopied by a magnolia tree. Here Eva fiddled with the band of a straw hat, while my mother sat and rested.

'Are you pleased we came?' said Eva.

'Yes, very …' said my mother.

'This is exactly how I imagined it would be.'

'And it's so quiet and peaceful.'

I followed the pathway that circled the well and headed towards a corner which dipped into a swath of tiny blue flowers. These were bunched so tightly that I couldn't see the ground. But why did these flowers interest me? Then I realised it wasn't the flowers themselves but their scent. This was dry and very sweet. Where had I come across this scent before, I wondered? I got down on my hands and knees and inhaled those blue flowers and then floated out lightweight with the proof of it.

45. New Faces, New Places

Random Thoughts And Themes – phenomenology. What happens doesn't matter, it's what we think of what happens that is important.

There were seventy-six casualties from the fire, only two made it to soft, creamy ashes – Vile and a tree squirrel. I have this image of the two of them – man and animal, hand in paw, grinning and squeaking into the kind flames.

Now I've said Vile didn't make it but that's not strictly true. The fact of the matter is I just don't know. The fire brigade stopped the fire at the seventeenth floor, I know that. And at some point Vile glided across the roof and poured smoothly like one of his home-made malts down the neck of the building, I know that too. I also know that two bodies were found in the charred piling and identified as Webley and Lenny. This gave the Putney Police something to chew over and consequently, I had a total of four interviews with them, because they were sure I could tell them what happened. But what could I say?

46. Over the Hills and Far Away

Random Thoughts And Themes – going away. Strike tents. Saddle up. Beetle off. Vamoose.

I hear a latch slipping back. A door opening. Purposeful steps. Then a man's voice. Indistinct bass tones. Now a woman's voice. Sharp, short syllables. She is answering his questions. Then a door bangs shut. Do I hear a woman's laughter? Silence. A lorry streams by in the distance, its powerful engine thudding like a fist. Silence again. I hear someone coughing. Coughing on what? An iron gate squeaks open. My stomach makes a sound (it doesn't want to be left out). More voices murmuring in the thickness of the night ...

Maurice and I are in Australia. We're about 15 miles outside Brisbane, in a tiny place called Cooroy, staying in a hotel full of musical plumbing, pay TVs and beautiful paintings of the desert.

We've come Big Name hunting for Maurice's MA thesis on prosthetics. For not far from where we are staying is a prosthetics museum of a unique kind – *temporary prosthethics*. They've got legs made out of broomsticks, chicken's eggs for eyeballs, fingers of papier-mâché. It's unbelievable!

Travelling with Maurice is good fun. He never stops talking. Though that's an advantage as far as I am concerned, because he always has something interesting to say. For example, on the plane, for the whole twenty-hour flight, Maurice regaled me with stories about his relatives. These were a seriously cuckoo crew. One that sticks in my mind is Uncle Ted, a cinema projectionist, who when he became stressed, opened and closed his mouth like a projector's film gate and fluttered his eyelids at twenty-four frames per second. Priceless.

Lots of things were destroyed in the fire, including my chair. Yes, the old glitz-trolley bought it. Sad, because I'd grown it from a standing start. Yet we'd been in Australia only three days when we discovered a motorised wheelchair club just down the street from where we were staying. I'm not kidding you, they had chairs sporting big 450cc four-cylinder pro modified engines. Engines that were turboed, quad carbed and running not on petrol but methanol. Yet that wasn't all. Apparently, they had a whole network of motorised wheelchair clubs across the country – regular race meets, competitions, TV coverage, the lot. I'm beginning to warm to this place. I really am.

From my bed I stare across the room and out through the window into the evening sky. Stars are everywhere. The moon is high too, huge and a deep gold colour. And when I gaze at it I feel sad, because it makes me think of my friends – Ishmael, Bim, Four-wheel-drive … Then as I look out into that night sky the stars seem to slide and cluster – the Bull, the Plough, the Crab? No – the grin! The whole of the night sky is suddenly ablaze with stars in the shape of an enormous, pulsing, evil-looking grin. I know that grin, I say to myself. I know that grin!